Each Day Is A Life

EACH DAY IS A LIFE

By Dave Borland

Elderberry Press

Elderberry Press
www. elderberrypress.com

Publisher's Catalog—in—Publication Data
Each Day Is A Life / Dave Borland

ISBN 13: 978-1-934956-82-3

1. Visionary & Metaphysical—Fiction.
2. Philisophical Movements / Humanism—Fiction.
3. Friendship—Fiction.
4. Political Movements / Peace—Fiction.
I. Title

To Families for support and encouragement.

CHAPTER ONE

At a certain point in life, one must reflect on past experiences and plan for the future. Mark Gentry had come to that belief. He was currently at that juncture, contemplating his next steps as he gazed out at the ocean waves. This was a crucial moment in his life, as he wanted to ensure that he was living life to the fullest by the time it came to an end. Although he had lived a solitary life without family ties, he had no regrets and was content with his choices.

Mark admired the natural beauty of the sky and the sea as the sun broke through the clouds. He walked along the beach, feeling the wind whistle past him and his hat flap in the breeze. Mark was proud of his walking prowess, which was all that remained of his once-powerful athletic skills, and he knew that he must stay in good shape if he was going to make the most of his time in this world.

Suddenly, a man on a three-wheeled bike whizzed past him, barely missing him. The man, who Mark mentally dubbed 'Captain No Neck,' appeared oblivious to others around him as he sped along the sand. Mark watched as the man disappeared into the distance, reflecting on how everyone had their own unique way of living their lives.

As he continued walking, Mark's mind was filled with thoughts about how to make the most of the remaining years of his life. He could see storm clouds approaching in the distance, a reminder that life was never calm for long. Nonetheless, he remained determined to make the most of his time and ensure that he experienced all that life had to offer.

As Mark walked along the beach, he saw two young women chatting and walking toward him. He'd often noticed how many women talked too much for his taste and shared their inner thoughts too freely. He didn't have anyone to share his thoughts with and as he past them, he kept a neutral expression on his face, like Asian actors in movies. He considered himself a nice guy but had no friends to confirm or deny this belief.

As he strolled along the beach, his feet sank into the soft sand, surrounded by a multitude of tiny shells. Each one was more beautiful than the last, with unique shapes and colors. The beauty of nature mystified him, and he gazed out at the swirling, white-capped ocean. The horizon was a perfectly straight line where the green water met the sky.

Suddenly, he checked his watch and realized he had to hurry back. He was meeting someone he hadn't seen in years, and it was bound to be a difficult conversation. Before he headed back to his cottage, he looked down the length of the beach, wishing he had time to walk further down it, but he would have to save that for later. He started his return walk to his cottage behind the grove of palmetto trees surrounding his ancient, 19th-century fishing shack renovated into a beach house.

The sandy path between two beach cottages was filled with footprints that Mark carefully avoided as he walked. He was a man who always kept to himself, both in his personal life and in his work. He preferred not to leave an impression on others, whether it be through his actions or words. Even in his line of work, where he dealt with business leaders, he tried to remain as anonymous as possible.

Mark arrived at his small beach house, which he affectionately called his "shack." It was a one-story house, likely built in the 1930s, by people who made the long winter journey from places like Pennsylvania and New York to escape to the warm temperatures and sun of the coast. As he climbed onto the front porch with an ancient swing that swayed gently in the ocean breeze, pleasant memories flooded his mind of his childhood spent on his grandfather's farm near Pittsburgh. In today's world, where popularity was everything, he cherished the simple peace the swing on the porch brought him when he'd sit and look down the narrow path to the waves breaking on the beach.

Inside his beach house, Mark tried to turn on the gas stove, but it didn't work, so he turned on the cold-water spigot instead. He filled a red kettle halfway and plugged it into the electric socket. After pouring coffee from a can into a plastic paper filter, he waited for the water to boil.

Looking around the kitchen, Mark's mind went

back to times as a kid when he'd watched his mother rolling flour wet with water into a flat circle so that she could make the promised pumpkin pie, his favorite. He admired her strength and resilience despite life's challenges. The pot buzzed, and steam rose into the air as he poured the water over the coffee. Mark enjoyed few things in life more than coffee, and he needed a boost to prepare for his pending visitor, Trevor McBride. He went back out to front porch and plopped down on the swing with his coffee, waiting for Trevor to arrive.

Trevor McBride was a contradiction of a man. An attorney by trade now and a CIA officer by experience. Trevor had been Mark's partner during his last year in the service and had remained in the CIA for years before leaving and entering a financially and successful career as a lawyer. Trevor lived on a working farm and horse ranch that was his family's, who were very wealthy. He was an odd combination of being lethal as he had killed men in the line of duty in the CIA, but he was also a charming, handsome man. He'd been married three times to beautiful, wealthy women with whom he had created five children, all now successful in their own ways, except Richard, who Mark knew from day's when both were in Paris. Mark met him there and he was a favorite of his as Richard was trying to succeed as a painter, but he suffered from a drug-related illness. The last time Mark had seen Trevor was in Paris which was also the last time he'd seen Richard. He and Trevor were both trying to help Richard get help for his drug dependency, but before they'd been able to convince Richard to get the help he needed, he had died suddenly from an overdose. Ironically, his painting became very popular in Paris after he had passed away.

Trevor had been terribly affected by Richard's death. He had even written several times to thank Mark for trying to help Richard, which was unusual for him to express positivity, as he was a generally a very selfish person. But since then, Mark hadn't seen or heard from Trevor until the email he'd gotten two days ago about today's visit.

After Mark's was discharged from the service, he'd kept in touch with many of his associates from his military days, but only once a few years ago from Trevor. He and Trevor had worked a year together, working on many top-secret assignments with objectives in many associations and governments around the world for the United States. Down deep, Mark did not like him. He was a selfish, self-centered man who would do anything to promote himself and Mark always wondered how he handled his law career, but apparently, very well by his reputation. The one-time Trevor contacted him was years ago and it was a phone call about a company he represented. For a huge fee, he would give Mark inside information, which he refused abruptly which Trevor did not like. He never had heard from him since until this email he just received. During Mark's career, he had never taken advantage of any of the contacts he had from his past top-secret missions while in the service. However, his international experience while in the service had been very valuable to him as he found much business all over the world. His knowledge of foreign governments around the world had undeniably been a tremendous help to him in his four-decade-long career.

As he awaited the arrival of Trevor, Mark wondered

why in the hell Trevor had emailed him two days ago, stating he needed to see him immediately. In response to Mark's reply, Trevor only stated that it was serious and that he needed to see Mark. As he swung gently on his porch, looking out to the limb-strewn front yard of the cottage, he heard a car door slam behind the bushes by the street in front of the cottage. He got up and went to the entryway on the porch and saw the tall, wide-chested Trevor walking up the front walk. He immediately waved at him, and the tall, grey-haired man he had known for most of his lifetime waved back at him as he walked briskly down the walk toward him.

CHAPTER TWO

"Been a while, old buddy, since we talked," Trevor said, reaching out to shake Mark's hand.

Mark reached out and grasped the large, narrow hand of a man he didn't like. "Five years, I'd say," he replied as he stood back and waved the visitor into the beach house.

The tall, willowy man with solid gray hair, slowly walked into the living area with the black brick fireplace within a whitened stone wall facing out. He looked around the small living area with a dark tan leather sofa and two wide chairs on either side. A round coffee table was in front of the sofa, filled with magazines and newspapers.

Mark said, "Grab a seat. I have some coffee brewing, or I can get you some tea if you'd like. What's your pleasure?"

"Coffee will work, and make it black," Trevor replied, looking around before sitting down on the end of the sofa.

Mark went over to the counter and poured the hot water into another paper filter with coffee over a cup, filling the cup. He came back and gave the coffee to Trevor and sat down in one of the overstuffed leather chairs across from the sofa.

Oddly, neither spoke as they both took sips of coffee, then Trevor put his cup down and said, "Mark, you know you are a strange bird. You know that don't you?" he said with a tight, grave look in his eyes.

Mark smiled slightly and replied, "Thank you. Something I am very proud of, Trevor."

Trevor's face remained stoic as he said, "You may be in danger, my old friend!"

Mark never changed his expression as he took another sip of his coffee and responded, "So, what other news do you have for me, old friend?" Mark asked sardonically.

Trevor straightened up, smiled a bit, and replied, "You're still the same son of a bitch I've known all these years," as he paused, looked away, then back to Mark, who just kept looking at him steadily.

Trevor finally said, "Here I am coming all the way out to this dump on the Carolina shore to tell you that I know someone's gunning for you. That one mean son-of-a-bitch is still unhappy with some deal you set up for him a few years ago."

Mark kept his poker face on, but now it was because his face was frozen. He put down the coffee cup and asked carefully, "Which mean son-of-one-bitch, Trevor, are you referring to?"

Trevor's face lit up, and he began to chuckle as he replied, "If I were you, I would ask around about anyone with a rep for making guys he doesn't like disappear."

Mark responded immediately, "You're not me, thank God, but I have handled myself for years quite well. No one is going to make me disappear. If I'm going to disappear, it'll be because I want to."

Trevor looked at him like he was crazy as he said, "What the hell does that mean?"

"It means that only I control my life; only me."

Trevor smiled and said, "You know, the last time we were together in Paris, you acted like you were invincible. I know you were trying to help Richard, who you got along with better than me, for Christ's sake, but your attitude about your solo life really got to me. Those deals I had for you that we could have pulled off, But no, not you. You were too good to help me out," he paused then said, "there's something about how you said to me the last time we talked, and I had that great deal, 'that you, and only you control your destiny'. Some shit like that, got to me, old friend. Sounds like you still believe your own bullshit."

Mark replied, "I do, and you do. Everyone controls their own destiny, Trevor, even you, for what good that does humanity," he said, staring Trevor in the eyes.

"Screw you, you smart ass son of a bitch." Trevor got up, gave Mark a long look, then slowly said, "Just remember, you dumb bastard, I warned you," he said, looking down at the still-seated Mark. He added, "From what I've been told, this is a dude from years ago. He's not a Russian or an Islamic terrorist."

"That's comforting, old buddy," Mark replied sarcastically. "You had me a bit scared there for a few seconds," he said. He paused and asked, "Okay, if I may be so bold, who is after me?"

Trevor showed a hint of surprise, then said, "Can't tell you exactly, but one of my sources brought your name up from an intercepted conversation last week between a Swedish company and some rich dude in Saudi Arabia. Apparently, you hooked them up, and the Saudi guys took them for…two billion kroners or something like that, and this dude was blaming a middleman from Pittsburgh named Mark, something or other. 'I want that bastard,' were his exact words."

Mark smiled slowly and replied, "Truthfully, I thank you for the information, Trevor, but I know all about it, and the guy is full of shit." He paused and added, "Anything else?"

"Anything else. Jesus Christ, I came here to help you, and you asked me if there is anything else." He paused and said, "You, cocky son of a bitch," as he spun and headed for the door. He turned back again as Mark got up and said, "Just stay there and wait for some son-of-a-bitch to silence you… you dumb bastard." He moved to go, then paused again, and said, "You know something, I never liked you, never will. I thought I was helping you because of what you did for Richard, but Jesus Christ, you are amazing," he said as he turned and walked to the front door.

Mark walked after him slowly and said, "Don't get me wrong, I appreciate you telling me, but I guess you were feeling guilty about the several times I saved your ass, both that year I worked with you in D.C. and that time in Paris when I gave you a heads up that U.S. intelligence was penetrating the computer systems of the company you started working for as a legal guru. My warning saved your ass, and you never even thanked me. So, if you want to know, Trevor, when you contacted me that you were coming, I realized just how much I don't like you. Oddly enough, you're probably the only person I ever felt that way about. You're so self-centered…oh, shit, just get the hell out of here. Your whole life, you were always the privileged one or you thought you were. Me, I was just a farmer's son from Monongahela, PA."

Standing on the porch now, Trevor looked back at Mark with that smirky smile, the one that Mark always hated, as he replied, "You were, and you still are an asshole." He turned and walked down the sidewalk. As he reached the gate, he turned and yelled back to Mark, who stood on his front porch, "Won't see you again, that's for sure. Just remember who tried to warn you, you dumb shit, because if it's the guy I think it is, he's dangerous."

Mark stood on the porch and watched Trevor get into his car and disappear into the wooded landscape. As he stood there, he wondered if he should be concerned about what he'd been told. He hadn't heard any rumors within the online communications sites he watched or from any his sources. Several times in his career, he had received threats from disgruntled people and company heads. He usually handled it by contacting them directly and letting them vent, threaten, and posture for a while. Then, he was ready with a logical response for them once they'd gotten all their ire out by yelling at him, and he outlined what they had achieved while working together and how he'd taken them from big-time financial losses to huge profits. That reminder usually calmed them down fast. He had never felt in imminent danger of physical threat by any of them, though, so this information from Trevor did have him feeling somewhat concerned, if for no other reason that Trevor seemed to believe so strongly that there was danger. Still, he thought he knew the guy Trevor was referring to. If it was him, he had talked with the guy already several times in the days after the closing of the deal and hadn't gotten even a hint of the kind of threat Trevor had been warning him of. Whether it was him or not, he would have to contact him again to confirm that everything was resolved. Well, at least Trevor was gone. And now he needed to prepare for his next case, which was going to be a difficult one.

CHAPTER THREE

Mark stood on the narrow wooden front porch, gazing at the road Trevor had driven away on. After a while, he went back inside the old seaside cottage and walked towards the back door, which overlooked the ocean. As he stood there, he smiled and thought about the man who had just left, reflecting on the unequal balance of humanity in the world. Many people find it challenging to survive, take care of their families, and fulfill their responsibilities. Meanwhile, a small group of individuals have always managed to thrive on the resources provided by others. Throughout human history, these individuals have exploited others to sustain their own existence.

Mark reflected on the fact that some people can live comfortably due to their favorable circumstances, while others struggle to survive with limited opportunities. He recognized that he was fortunate to have had a supportive upbringing, education, athleticism, white skin, and other advantageous qualities that had contributed to his success.

Throughout his life, he had strived to balance his own personal pursuits with a desire to assist those in need. He had always held the belief that it was important to provide for oneself and for others who depend on them. As he contemplated his life's philosophy, he reminded himself that each day was an opportunity to live life to the fullest. This approach had proven successful for him over the years, and he felt content with where he was in life.

Mark stood and watched the waves curling up towards the beach. He believed that responsibility was the key to success. He spent his career settling disputes, even for wealthy clients, without resorting to violence. He was skilled in creating responsible outcomes that benefited both parties, many times without them even realizing it. If someone felt they were being treated unfairly, he always had a counter solution that highlighted their achievements and prevented them from suffering financially as bad as they might behave if they battled for all they wanted. He saw it as a game, much like his beloved sport of tennis, where he had a great backhand that usually led to victory. His goal was to achieve a positive outcome for both parties without causing major harm to anyone involved. He had never destroyed an organization, but rather resolved disputes respectfully and positively, so they were able to continue their business.

Throughout his career spanning several decades, he earned the nickname "The Fixer", for his usual ability to satisfy both parties involved in a negotiation. He would often smile to himself, finding his own sense of humor amusing and using it to stay relaxed. He felt proud of his moniker, as it accurately described his profession.

His business card featured a wrench turning a bolt, a symbol of his expertise. Reflecting on his life's work while gazing at the tranquil ocean waves, he chuckled to himself, pleased with his commitment to treating everyone fairly and positively, especially those who may have faced hardships if they lost out drastically in their dispute.

As he pondered these familiar thoughts, his attention turned to his own life. He had no family or close friends, but he considered himself to be the most content person he knew.

He shook himself to free himself from that train of thought and headed to the kitchen. He filled the coffee pot with water and added three scoops of dark coffee to the filter - caffeine was his only addiction. While waiting for the water to boil, he walked back to the long window and admired the view of the ocean. He realized the ocean needed a walk from him, but he had work to do first.

Mark's laptop was an integral part of his life. It contained information about everything he had done, and all the ongoing jobs and current offers he had from people all over the earth asking for him to settle their disputes. Mark poured coffee into his cup and went to the dining table, a ten-foot-long oak slab that worked double duty as his dining table and desk. He sat down and turned on his computer and dual screens. Reflexively, he checked the weather for the week. Then the national news, which was disappointing, as usual. Mark didn't usually pay much attention to it because he was disheartened by the financial-oriented, impersonal society that had taken over not just the United States, but the whole world. This belief had begun to trouble him because he was a part of this financial whirlpool that controlled the world. Over the past year, he had seriously considered quitting his job because his personal beliefs had drastically changed. The world was now being controlled by social media and artificial intelligence, including himself. He had wealth and personal peace, but he believed that the world was heading towards some type of destructive conflict. He needed to get out, but he had to complete some professional commitments first.

Mark opened his work files and tried to make some progress on his current case. However, he found it difficult to focus as his mind was occupied with thoughts of retiring from his one-man operation after almost fifty years. The things Trevor had told him, about someone who apparently had a grudge against him, further distracted him. As he stared at the computer screen, he realized that everyone, regardless of where they were, was trying to sell something—usually themselves. This realization troubled him as he had been doing the same thing for years.

His thoughts then drifted back to his childhood when he was an avid baseball player in high school and college. Despite being a well-built boy, he was often picked on by bullies because he never sought friends, but if they came after him, he managed to overpower them without throwing a single punch. Oh, they'd thrown some at him, but he'd invariably caught them, quickly twisting them into a pretzel before letting them go. They would run away to fake their toughness to their classmates, bragging that they'd taken Mark down even though they themselves had been thoroughly defeated.

Mark had let them say what they wanted. He despised bad language, bullies, and those who took advantage of others, and still did even as an adult. As a man who spoke six languages, Mark had a knack for detecting people's true intentions after only a few words, which had often revealed their dishonesty.

CHAPTER FOUR

While sitting at his laptop, he mulled over Trevor's warning about a possible threat to his life. As he had been thinking, he wasn't really concerned, because of the few people who seemed to be upset about the settlement in the last few years, he thought all had recognized how good his work had been by salvaging what could have a disaster. This thought particularly struck him because Sweden held immense importance to him, having been where he had begun his work with his very first job. As years passed, he'd made it his European base and had a well-established system in place there. Trevor's words made him consider possibilities of people in Sweden who might bear a grudge against him, but no one came to mind. The guy he had thought of had come around, so he couldn't figure out who Trevor was talking about.

Over the years, he had dealt with several unsavory individuals who owned companies worth billions, or sometimes just millions. Some of them were unhappy with the outcomes he had arranged for them. However, he had always made sure that they knew they were lucky to have him. He had saved many of them from bankruptcy. There were a few hidden entrepreneurs from Eastern Europe and Middle Eastern countries who were particularly unpleasant characters, but they were far from being Swedish. Mark paused and tried to recall the names of the worst offenders with the most adverse outcomes. He jotted down the names that came to his mind on his trusty yellow pad. As he did so, his computer dinged, and he glanced at the screen.

Mark's website, called "HANDSHAKES," had two new situations for him to handle. He received requests to intervene and follow-ups on cases he had already decided on. However, ninety-five percent of the situations he received were not related to his work and were deleted. The remaining five percent were from people or companies who seemed knowledgeable about his field. Mark carefully reviewed all the potential cases and diagnosed them, like how a doctor would before deciding on surgery. He was down to four companies and two cases, and after an hour of reviewing these cases, he sent out acceptance notifications.

He took a break and made himself a couple of peanut butter and apple butter sandwiches with cottage cheese, which was his favorite lunch combination. When he checked back to his online site, he was surprised that all four companies had responded and accepted his proposal. He immediately informed them that he would work on their cases and would set up the meeting place and time. Then he sat with another cup of coffee and reviewed all the back data sent to him weeks before by these companies, which would be his focus for the day.

The first dispute concerned a software company called Silver Lining, situated in Seattle, Washington, which used DNA data to locate missing persons across the globe, primarily in the Western world. The company was owned by a woman named Maggie Sutherland. The other company was in London, named Piccadilly Plus, had somehow obtained her unique system or one that was very similar to it through black data methodology. Piccadilly Plus, owned by an immigrant from India, claimed that they had developed and patented the system, and that there were many differences to Silver Lining's system. However, Silver Lining's system was exceptional as it could translate information and compare data with everything available online, including all social media systems worldwide. Since a legal ruling would take years, they decided to have Mark settle the situation. Although Mark believed that a merger was the best solution, he knew that was a discussion to approach later in the mediation proceedings. He would think more about this one before deciding, but would set up a meeting next week, as they needed an answer.

The other situation involved TR Enterprises, based in Leningrad, and created by Tomasic Romonoff, who had developed a method of using sonic beams to turn garbage into fuel. However, the other company was in Oslo called Norway Universal that claimed they'd had the same system for ten years, which TR denies.

Over the past weeks, amongst other possible situations, Mark had gathered information on all four of the companies; business data from them; their financials; their business reputations; and their legal or corporate, non-legal disagreements, which he believed could either lead to warfare or a mutually agreed upon settlement. After negotiating with all four companies and exchanging email messages and data, they agreed to have Mark intervene preliminarily if he decided to do so, which he could tell they really wanted. Now that he had chosen them and they had accepted his proposal, Mark would begin to set up a meeting between the parties in Paris, which was a perfect neutral location to settle the situation and avoid legal and literal warfare. Both parties knew that their existence was at stake, and Mark was confident he could work out a solution that everyone could live with. He would set up both for Paris next week.

Within an hour Mark received email messages back from representatives of all four companies and they all agreed on Paris for the sessions. He had been invited to visit their respective headquarters in Seattle, London, Moscow, and Oslo, but as always, he declined. Mark sat back as he read their emails and wondered how he could coordinate these meetings in Paris in less than a week. Normally, if he had more than one settlement, he would separate them by three days, say next Tuesday and Friday. He would start immediately to secure the meeting locations, hotels nearby, and restaurant reservations the night of the signing of the agreements, where he always paid for the final mediation dinner after agreements had been reached.

Mark traveled alone without any supporting personnel, just his trusty iPhone and laptop. Both devices were equipped with top-notch security software and cloud backup, ensuring maximum protection. Within three hours, even with the hour difference in Paris, he efficiently arranged all the necessary details for his upcoming meetings including accommodations, dinner reservations and conference room in his favorite hotel in Paris. Depending on the companies' preferences, he may need to visit their location before the settlement conference, once agreed upon and signed, but he plans to remain in constant contact with all four of them via his computer and cell phone.

After creating a plan for a major project, he realized he had to leave the beach house immediately and head back to Pittsburgh before departing for Paris. He contacted his private valet service, owned by Sol Weinberg, an ex-Marine and one of the few Jewish Marines he had ever met. Ironically, Sol was also a Pittsburgher, growing up In Squirrel Hill, the Jewish suburb. Sol was a rarity as a Jew in the Marines but also one of the toughest Marines he had ever encountered. They first met in Lebanon when Mark was twenty-four and assigned to a Marine intelligence unit for several months the year he worked with Trevor. During a reconnaissance mission, he was assigned to work with Sol to find two ex-Marines who were thought to have sold out their country for millions of dollars. A Saudi Prince was attempting to undermine the Lebanese government and needed legitimate undercover agents to do so. The two ex-Marines were perfect for the plot, having been attached to the American legation as part of a security force. Sol and Mark jointly stopped the explosion, arresting the two Marines who served long sentences. From that first meeting, Mark and Sol had become close friends, which was rare for Mark. As he reminisced about the exciting and dangerous last year of his military service, he thought about how ironic it was that Trevor showed up just as he was about to leave for Paris where he spent time with Trevor and his son had died,

As he packed his belongings, he couldn't help but think of his friend Sol. Despite the odds being against him, Sol had built a successful life for himself. After leaving the Marines, he settled in D.C. and started a driving service with only one vehicle and himself as the driver. Over the years, the business had grown into a national and international special and what he called a personal driving service run by his daughters now in all the major cities of the world for businesspeople with money. Sol became a millionaire about five times over during his years of starting and expanding the business. When he retired Sol moved back into the old house his parents had in Squirrel Hill in Pittsburgh. When Mark was in Pittsburgh, Sol, in his late sixties, would personally drive his old friend Mark anywhere he needed to go until he could no longer drive, which was just before he passed away. Now, one of Sol's female drivers located up in the Wilmington office was on her way to pick up Mark from his beach retreat in an hour to take him to the airport. He would be heading to Pittsburgh first, and then to Paris by dinner time tomorrow. As he reminisced about Sol, he smiled when he remembered how his friend had asked him several times over the years if he had a lady somewhere. Sol himself, had married a beautiful lady taller than him, who bore him three children, and he believed Mark needed a companion in his life. Mark always remembered his replies to Sol and numerous people over the years, stating that he was fine alone and didn't want to hold any woman back from having the life she wants. Sol's only disagreement over the years was that Mark needed someone by his side. As he thought about his old friend, now gone, it saddened him.

Mark had had several wonderful relationships with women over the years, but none that ever led to a life together. This was mostly because the women he dated were more independent than he was, especially Rebecca McKee. Rebecca was a lady ten years his junior, with her own successful business in the travel industry. After a twenty-year off and on relationship with Mark, she had finally given up on him and moved to Australia. Mark still talked to her on their cell phones, but she seemed happy with her new life down under.

Looking back, all of Mark's relationships were with independent women. When they ended things, it was a win-win for everyone involved. Did Mark want children? Not really. He has always loved and respected children, and he had secretly sponsored many kids in various programs on his travels around the world. Early on, he realized that he was a selfish person. His selfishness was so intense that he knew it would negatively impact any woman he lived with and had children with. Ironically, Mark's most successful work relationships had been with women. They worked together well because there isn't any male-female drama going on when they had a job to complete. Mark's work was defined by the two words "correct as planned."

CHAPTER FIVE

Mark arrived in Pittsburgh at midnight, right on schedule. As he approached the airport gate where cabs were lined up, he headed for Sol's Transpo Service, where he was greeted with a warm smile from Dominick, their top driver in the city. Dominick, a Polish man from the Southside of Pittsburgh, had been a friend of Mark's for years. Mark, a history enthusiast, was familiar with the rich history of the city, often comparing his knowledge to that of a devout Christian and their knowledge of the Bible. Dominick, however, had always been perplexed by his non-Polish first name, given to him by his grandmother, who had raised him strictly after his mother's death and father's abandonment. As they drove across the Fort Pitt Bridge, the city's glowing skyline and the convergence of the three rivers was a breathtaking sight, especially on such a clear night.

"Nice to see you, Bud. Twice this month, that's a record," Dom said.

"Well, had the annual checkup here as you know

and had some great days at the beach, but had to come back for just a half day to get some data I left up at my Mt. Washington office. We'll go up there tomorrow morning, before I go to the airport, if you can work that into your schedule, Dom."

"No problem. What time?"

"Nine bells will do it, Dom," as Mark paused and said, "Hey, the Bucco's getting better I see."

"Finally got some dudes that can hit, for Christ's sake. Baseball was born to hit the ball. You know what I mean?" he replied.

"I do," Mark replied with a smile crossing his broad face.

They pulled up to the Omni William Penn Hotel, or what was once just the William Penn, an oldline hotel in the middle of the city that had always been his favorite place to stay in this city. Dominick was out quickly and pulled his bag from the trunk, setting it on the sidewalk. "Well, I'll see you right here in the AM tomorrow, old buddy and I'll get you to the airport."

Mark slipped him a fifty-dollar bill and said, "Okay, make it eight-thirty instead of nine. Need a quick trip up to Mt. Washington for just a few minutes, then you can buzz me out to airport, okay?"

"Got 'cha," Dominick replied as he closed the door and came around, climbing back into dark, gray car. Without looking up at Mark, he just waved his left hand out the window and pulled away.

Mark watched him going down Grant Street, then picked up his bag and headed into the hotel. He took a quick shower and was in bed in a few minutes. He fell asleep immediately and woke up to light pouring in through his window. Rolling over he saw the time was close to 7:30, which was late for him, and he had to meet Dominick at 8:30. It took him a half hour to do his morning routine and as he finished shaving his lightly haired face, his cell phone beeped. Wiping his face quickly, he headed for the table next to his bed where his beeping phone was going through a catatonic fit.

"Yep," Mark grunted into the phone, standing in his underwear. He stood listening for almost a minute before responding, "You have to be shitting me," was his first and only response as his face tightened. For another minute he stood with the phone on his ear before saying gruffly, "I'll call back tomorrow," and terminated the call. For a minute he just stood there stunned, and then slowly sat down. Sitting in his jockey shorts and t-shirt, Mark's face was frozen. He sat there for minutes without moving.

"What the hell am I going to do now," he finally muttered out loud. As he ran his right hand over his face, he stood up and walked to the window that looked out over the city of his youth. For the first time in ages, his life possibly was not only in danger, but his vocation, or better put, his life's work status was literally over, also. He stood there, stunned. 'What do I do now?', he thought again in a daze. He let out a short laugh of disbelief.

The week before departing for his beach vacation, he underwent a thorough examination from his regular primary care physician, Dr. Jerome Whitaker at the University Hospital in Oakland. Mark had been visiting Dr. Whitaker annually for many years and the tests were always uneventful, except for some occasional high blood pressure readings which he was able to reduce through a diet change and yoga practices. When he received a call from Dr. Whitaker' primary nurse, Sheila, he was shocked to learn that an ultrasound of his pancreas, showed a growth, along with a high PSA level in blood work that could indicate a cancerous growth in his pancreas. Dr. Whitaker wanted him to undergo an immediate MRI and other extensive tests. Mark was initially frozen with disbelief, as he had never expected to be confronted with such a diagnosis. After taking a moment to collect himself, Mark poured a couple shots of scotch from the hotel bar set-up and sat down on the sofa, to process the news, staring blankly at the TV screen filled with local news.

CHAPTER SIX

Mark was always conscious of his health, carefully choosing his food and regularly engaging in exercises like walking and yoga to keep his mind and body in top shape. So, the news he received from the phone call left him devastated. Gradually, though, his mind began to calm down and analyze the situation, as it usually did when he faced challenges related to his role in overseeing two companies' financial and leadership matters. This time, however, he had to focus on a problem that affected his own existence. As he looked at the time, he realized it was almost 8:30 and quickly reached for his phone to call Dominick, who picked up on the first ring.

"Change of plans, Dom. Big change. Listen, I'm not leaving yet. Just go about your business and I'll get back to you when I know what I'm doing. Sorry, old buddy." He listened for a few seconds and then snapped his phone shut.

He sat back on to his bed. After a minute of just thinking what he had to do, he realized he had two calls to make. Sweden, for sure, but first New York, to the woman, Marsha McDonough, who had given him this contract settlement to solve and then Stockholm,

Mark looked at the clock. "Almost nine here and three in the afternoon in Stockholm, so I should call Marsha in New York first" he muttered to himself. He picked up his cell phone and tapped in numbers. It took only seconds for it to ring. "Marsha, here," came the response in a deep, resonant female voice.

"It's me, Mark."

Marsha McDonough's workplace was a two-story, brick building built in the 1880's situated behind Flatbush Avenue in Brooklyn. Previously, Marsha had spent her entire career in Manhattan, but things took a different turn when she faced a near-death experience on 9/11. Her office floor collapsed, and she lost all her co-workers in the tragedy. Fortunately, Mark, who worked with her at the time, had called her to meet him at an office overlooking Central Park, where a billionaire entrepreneur had shown interest in purchasing a company through her. Mark acted as the middleman, and the deal proved to be fruitful for Marsha three years later, when business had resumed its pace after the disaster. Marsha never forgot the incident and remained grateful to Mark, who, in a way, had saved her life. She created most of the business sessions he ended up moderating at "The Fixer". Marsha in a way had made him what he was.

"What's up, old timer. You on your way to Stockholm?"

"No, I got a plan for that, but decided on the two others you sent me last month. My plan was to do them at the same time in Paris, where I set up separate meetings already. You sent me the companies and were hyper about getting It done and I think I have a good plan for both, but that's why I'm calling. Ran into a hitch."

"Oh, the ones I've been pestering you about. Well, that's great news. The ones you were trying to figure out how to handle them. Terrific, but what's the problem?" Marsha asked.

Mark responded, "Never have I had this kind of problem before in my life."

"You're getting married to a twenty-year-old cheerleader, is that it?"

"It's a bit more than that, Marsha," he calmly replied. Mark, speaking quietly, related the call he received from his doctor's office and explained that he had to have tests done immediately to determine how critical was the cancer discovered in his pancreas and if it had metastasized.

She didn't respond immediately but he could hear her breathing for a few seconds. Then she said brusquely, "Get your ass to him, now."

Mark was surprised by her emphatic response. He paused before saying, "I'm supposed to go to Paris today for the four companies you sent me. I have a plan for them which I will send to you immediately, but I know that your number one concern is the Swedish problem. I know this will solve your Swedish problem that you need desperately, without me even being there."

Marsha said strongly, "You never give up, do you," she paused and then said, "OK, what do you got?"

"Get them together on your system and explain, if you want, my situation, but tell them I came up with a solution to their situation," as Mark paused and added, "But you have to use the word, win. Capital WIN.'"

"Win. What the hell does that mean?" she quickly responded.

"Last week I talked to them both. They are ten percent away from an agreement. Both are standing on the edge of a cliff that is about to collapse which means that both are close to falling into the canyon below, because they are both stubborn and rich. That's a bad combination but below, or I should say above them, on the top of the mountain is Tao Cheng, who will take over the whole worldwide distribution of this interstellar communicative system if these two jagoffs continue to fight each other. I know they now have the capability to control the current and future communication system that will dominate this world. But only if they come together—or Cheng will. They can dominate, but only if they come together. Again, explain my situation, but tell them this is my solution."

Marsha interjected, "Great bullshit, Mark. Are you going into politics? I want to know if you can bring these bastards together or not, but more importantly, how?"

"Only if you tell them to accept," he paused, then said, "win, all capitals, WIN?"

"What is this win bullshit," she paused and added, "I know you got a major medical problem, but with this deal, you've lost it, after all these years. So, I'm hanging up. Get your test done now, goddamn it. Oh, and your payment up to this moment will be transferred and don't bother me again until you call me with what the doctors say," she said.

Immediately Mark interjected, "World International Network."

Her line stayed open and then she said, "What's that?"

"That, my ex-old friend, is what I will be sending both online as soon as you buzz off. It is a super satellite generated system that will dominate communications not only on this Earth, but way up above the clouds for future generations, no matter where man decides to land."

"WIN," she said quietly. "Who has it and when can it begin to operate?"

"Max has close to half of the technology and Ivan the other. Give up a bit and take a lot. Create WIN in Stockholm or here in my hometown, Pittsburgh, for Christ's sake. It will make no difference." He paused, then asked, "Well, do I send it to them as soon as you go bye-bye?"

Marsha quickly replied, "Send it. If they buy, I buy," and she paused and added softly, "I hope your tests work out. You are one goddamn genius, and I love and hate you at the same time." as she paused and said bluntly, "Get those tests done. Much love."

"Okay, about Paris. I have everything set up for both. I am going to send this to you right now and you are going to structure it for them, then send it immediately. I will talk to them with the truth of my situation and explain what they are getting separately is a perfect solution for them. Read what I will send you. Go there yourself, if you want, but it is laid out simply but financially positive for all four companies. I would put it off a day or so and you go if you are up to it. If by chance my doctors let me go, I will go in a day or so. But explain to each boss my dilemma. I have talked to them, one on one and I know they trust me and will trust you. Give it a shot. I will go in two days if I am allowed, or you go and give them my solution." He stopped and waited for her response.

There was none, then she replied, "I will go. Send it all to me, but you go to that doctor now," she bellowed over the phone.

Mark replied, "This will work, and I am so proud of you, Marsha. They will love you. You'll get the WIN deal and the Paris deals. Me, I'll get the pancreas deal."

"Send it now and I will call them. I'll stay with Paris. Send me all your schedules and reservations. I'll take my daughter, Betsy with me. She's good and has always had a crush on you, for some ungodly reason. Just send that stuff to me and go see the doc," and hung up.

He immediately pulled up Marsha's name in the text app and tapped in, "Enclosed are all my work for the Swedish WIN deal and the Paris companies. Go get 'em, Marsha. Oh, a big favor. You remember that guy I knew way back, Trevor, who worked with the CIA years ago. He stopped by my beach house and said that one of my old clients wanted to do me in. Something about he thought I screwed him over. Can you check on who that might be? Between my pancreas and this guy, I'm not long for this world." He put his phone down and tapped all the files for the WIN and his proposals for the four companies meeting in Paris.

He sat back and thought, "Wow, so much already and I still have to see my doctors, but first have to talk to my Paris companies."

CHAPTER SEVEN

Mark anxiously waited in the chair after completing his new tests. It was early afternoon and he felt frozen, anticipating the results of the tests he'd taken. His eyes drifted to a window, where he gazed across the Monongahela River to Mount Washington, admiring the beautiful weather. However, his personal situation did not match the sunny day. Suddenly, his phone vibrated. He retrieved it from his vest pocket and noticed Marsha's name on the screen. He quickly answered the call.

"Hey, what's up?"

"Sorry to bother you, Mark. Any news yet?" Marsha quietly asked.

"No, still waiting for the doc. Should be out shortly. I guess he's going over all the results. Christ, I was tested for so much, just don't know what to expect."

"Let me know as soon as you can. Oh, by the way, they bought WIN."

Mark smiled slightly and replied, "They had to, but thanks for sticking with me."

"I was bluffing before. You know that?", Marsha responded.

"I knew. You can't live without me," he paused, "hopefully you won't have to."

Marsha continued, "Another thing, the guy who was mouthing off about what you set up for him, was a Turk, named Erogan, who had those oil fields that we hooked up with the French company, EurOil. That was three years ago, and he thought his deal was bad, now that oil has gone up so much, which you had nothing to do with. My external contact guy, whom you know, ex-CIA, had a talk with him and he now understands. So don't worry about that dude, just fix that pancreas of yours. Oh, I talked with the four companies. They received all your data and look forward to meeting me in Paris. I think it's still going to work. Can't believe you put so much together and to me, it looked terrific. Thanks, and I hope your tests are okay. Please let me know. I'm leaving in an hour but call me when you can".

"I'll know in a few minutes as the nurse just came in. Thanks for taking care of the Paris and the Turk," and Mark snapped shut his phone.

Louise, or "Lou," his nurse and Dr. Whitaker's chief nurse came up to him with a handful of papers in a blue plastic folder. She had become a friend over the years, mostly because she was a Pirate fanatic, as lousy as they had been in recent years. They would laugh and joke about the Bucco's, but there was no laughter on her face as she walked up to him now.

"Whadda you got for me, Lou?" Mark said with a bit of bravado.

Her face didn't change as she came up to him and

sat down on a small, leather covered bench beside him.

"Mark, you want to go get a cup of java down the hall?" she said in a serious tone.

"You buying?", he came back with his usual, sly smile.

"Never happen, money man," she responded quickly, as she turned and walked down the long, narrow hallway with Mark keeping up with her brisk pace. They arrived at the cafeteria without saying a word, they joined the line to order. In a few minutes Mark was carrying a tray with two coffees and several muffins as Lou headed towards a quiet corner table with a window.

Mark set down the tray and took a seat across from Lou. They both sipped their coffee in silence, enjoying the peace away from the busy hospital. Lou eventually put down her cup and retrieved a blue folder from her bag. She opened it and began to review a set of papers.

"Okay, let's get to it," she said. She looked at the folder and then looked up at Mark. She spoke was a deep, yet soft voice, filled with conviction. Each word was carefully enunciated, and her manner of speaking was like that of a preacher addressing their congregation. Lou was an intelligent middle-aged woman who had endured a difficult upbringing and marriage, but still managed to excel in her class at Pitt despite being ten years older than her peers. She completed college in just two and a half years and obtained her nursing degree in two years, both ahead of the expected timeline. Mark had known her for a decade, and she always provided straightforward explanations of Whitaker's medical decisions, which had been minor in his case over the years. However, this time, her delivery was straightforward and different as she leaned over and said, "Mark, what I can say is that this is not good. You had all your tests, and the doctor knows you were set to leave town, but he wants you to stick around today, because he has already contacted Pittsburgh Surgery for his best friend, Dr. Conrad Dillinger, to supervise an MRI with the Oncology Unit. What he led me to believe, and you will hear it from him when you go over there in a few minutes, is that somehow this thing is much more than he thought."

"What is this thing, Lou?"

"A cancerous growth that is literally choking the shit out of your pancreas."

"Why haven't I felt something, for Christ's sake," Mark asked in a surprisingly calm voice.

"You probably have. But knowing you, you probably thought you had eaten something or some other typical reaction that comes from guys," Lou responded. "The point, buster, is that what you got is pretty deadly. Doc told me to tell you that time is not on your side, but there are some new treatments they want to talk to you about," she stopped, looked up at the wall clock and went on, "in about a half hour."

Mark looked at Lou without any reaction on his face. He turned and looked up at the clock and then back to Lou and said slowly, "Whew, a bit too much, love," he replied as he looked away from her as if drifting off to some other world. He stayed silent and frozen. He remained this way as Lou looked away and her right hand went up to her cheek, wiping away a tear. Finally, he turned to her and reached over, picking up her hand. He took his other hand and gently massaged her hand as he looked at her wettened eyes. "It's okay, Lou. It's okay. We'll do something, I know … something."

She looked at him as a slight smile came across her face as their hands stayed clasped. Then she said, "We will, Mark, but it's going to be tough." She squeezed his hands and said, "You know that me and the doc will be with you every second."

Mark took hold of her and hugged her tightly, eyes closed. Tears were in both their eyes as he slowly pushed back, looked at her and said, "I know, I know, I know. Wouldn't want anyone else in my corner for this fight."

They picked up their trays and dropped them off at the entrance to the cafeteria and walked slowly, without talking, back to the office. As they walked into the office area, she pointed to a chair and Mark went over and sat down. "Sit there and I'll get Dr. Whitaker."

It was less than a minute later when the door opened, and Dr. Whitaker was standing there with another doctor in a white jacket behind him. Dr. Whitaker waved at Mark to come with him as he turned and went back through the door. Mark got up and followed him, Lou, and the other doctor, down the narrow hallway into an examination room. He walked in and sat down as the two doctors stood in their white jackets both holding paperwork and Lou closed the door.

Mark looked up at the two doctors as Dr. Whitaker said, "Mark, this is Dr. Conrad Wisnewski, who is our specialist in treating cancer of the pancreas." Dr. Wisnewski came over and reached over to Mark. They shook hands as Dr. Whitaker walked over to a vacant sofa and sat down.

Lou got up and started for the door, but Dr. Whitaker put his hand up and said, "Lou, please stay. You're going to be a big help in seeing what we can do for Mark." She came over and sat down next to Dr. Whitaker as Dr. Wisnewski remained standing.

It was silent for a few seconds, then Mark said calmly, "Okay, what, is the game plan, assuming there is one?"

Dr. Wisnewski looked over to Dr. Whitaker who smiled and said, "Okay, let me give you a summary and then Dr. Wisnewski will outline a plan he has for you." He talked for a few minutes, in his quiet, efficient, yet concentrated way about the tests that had been done. Then he asked Dr. Wisnewski to summarize what he saw in the test results and what he thought they could do to slow and hopefully reduce the cancer.

Wisnewski was a big man with wide shoulders, a dark triangular beard on his chin and brilliant blue eyes. His voice was deep, yet soft and as he talked to Mark, he never took his eyes off him. His inflections were clear, yet gentle, as he detailed in layman's terms the seriousness of Mark's situation. The bottom line, he slowly explained was that they needed to immediately begin treatment in order to first, stop the cancer's current activity and second, to try to reduce the chances of the cancer from spreading elsewhere.

They talked quietly for a while until Mark straightened up in his chair, and with a set face, said, "How much time, doc's?"

Whitaker looked at Wisnewski, then leaned towards Mark, "Not much, Mark, not much. We need to start immediately to try and stop this from spreading."

"How much, Doc?"

"Months, probably," Whitaker replied.

Mark's eyes didn't blink, and his face remained stoic, then he turned toward the window that looked out over the Monongahela River. He could see Mt. Washington clearly in a distant, spectacular setting from a brilliant morning sun. So many times, as a kid, his dad would take him for rides all over the city, and his favorite was riding along Grandview Avenue, looking out over the city. They always stopped and walked out to the overlook, and his dad would point out the landmarks down below in the downtown and along the Monongahela. His father had known everything about the city. As he looked out across the river and to the hill, realizing what he was facing, for the first time in decades he could feel tears building in his eyes. He kept looking at the hillside and his mind was filled with images of his dad's face, that ever-present slight smile crinkling his cheeks. Oh, how he wished his dad was there with him now.

"You okay, Mark?" Dr. Whitaker asked quietly as he laid a hand on his shoulder.

Mark turned back and said, "Just wandering back a bit," he replied, looking up at the narrow, firm face of Dr. Whitaker. Then he added, "Let's get on with it, doc."

CHAPTER EIGHT

Mark found himself in a pub on Pittsburgh's North Side a week later, watching English soccer and sipping on a dark porter. The Bystander, as the place was called, specialized in showing English soccer on its huge TV. Mark had been feeling down since leaving Dr. Whitaker's office a week ago. He had canceled his business meetings that had been scheduled months in advance and had been talking to Marsha once a day. Marsha was still shocked by what Mark had told her after his appointment with Dr. Whitaker. She had three cases lined up for him, plus the one in Paris, which somehow, she presented Mark's program, which they accepted. Now she was looking for another person to settle their differences since "The Fixer" was in his own predicament, as she had said to him sadly and quietly. In the following days, Mark was mostly in a daze. He spent his time in his hotel room or wandering around downtown Pittsburgh. He wasn't afraid of dying, but he felt alone. The only person who knew about his situation was Marsha, someone he respected, but who was as concerned about her profit than his well-being, which he understood. Mark had no family or close friends to tell his situation. No one knew about his situation or cared about him, except for Marsha, who he had made millions for over the years from his work.

Mark took a sip of his beer and looked around the pub. It was almost vacant as it was early in the afternoon. He looked up at the giant flat screen with teams from Manchester United and Arsenal battling in a 1-1 tie with eight minutes left in regulation play. As usual the chanting and singing from the overflow crowd coming from the stands could be heard and it was mesmerizing, almost as exciting as the players dexterity on the field. However, his thoughts returned to his personal problem. He was a wealthy seventy-year-old plus man with no one to spend his money on or leave it to when he passed away.

Mark looked down at his mug of beer, which had lost its head, and was now just a glass of brown beer. He looked around the pub again and it was now empty except for him at the bar and the tall, but brawny bartender owner who kept walking around getting the place ready for a hoped late afternoon influx. Mark was totally silent as he looked back up at the TV with a soccer match, a game he liked—because it involved normal-sized men or women competing in a non-stop game with little trickery but exceptional running and kicking skills. It was a game of sport he really enjoyed. He turned and looked down the bar to the bartender, who had introduced himself minutes ago, as Timothy McDonald, "Call me Tim," he had said.

Tim was now checking the bottles on the shelves which were on either side of the wide mirror and huge, TV above. After no talk between them, Tim turned toward Mark, came around the bar and sat down next to him. He put his foot up on the counter under the bar and they talked for a good half hour.

Tim went on to give him a background of the bar and himself, including a summary of his family. Tim was a fifth generation Scot whose family came to Pittsburgh in the early 1800's from Donegal. Mark was mesmerized by the young man because he was quiet, positive, and not inquisitive about the older man, him, sitting alone sipping on a dark porter which had lost its head. Mark didn't reveal anything about himself or his situation, just remained listening to the young man.

Finally, Tim said, "You hurting man?"

Mark looked away from Tim, then slowly turned to him sitting beside him. After a few seconds of just looking at each other he said to Tim, "Like I never have before."

Tim didn't respond for a few seconds, then he got up and walked around to the other side and took a mug off the counter next to the wall. He turned and stood in front of the line of taps with the draft beer. He stood there dumping the bland brown beer into the grill under the tap, then put the mug under the tap. In a few seconds a new dark beer filled the mug with the glass half-filled with a white head. He turned and came back to where Mark was sitting and slid it in front of him. "Give that a shot, man, it'll start you back."

Mark looked at him and a slow smile came to his face. He straightened up a bit and said, "Speaking of shots, how about laying your oldest Glenlivit on me, son."

Tim looked at him, turned and walked down the bar to the bottles on shelves beside the wide TV screen. He reached up for and pulled down a bottle with a Glenlivit label on it and picked up a shot glass, then walk around the end of the bar and came back to where Mark was sitting. He put the bottle and the shot glass right in front of him and started to pour from the bottle, then stopped and said, "You know, I'm going to hold off on this until I have a clue what's going through that percolating mind of yours."

Mark sat up and looked at the young man he'd just met whose job was to pour booze and make small talk, in his opinion. "You serious, son?"

"Son, you say; is that a demeaning response, old boy?"

Mark was at first a bit peeved by the young bartender, but then a smile creeped slowly onto his face as he replied, "I'm over seventy, you're maybe thirty, so to me you're a kid and someone's son. Me, I'm an old guy who's been sucking on a beer in your joint."

They stared at each other for a few moments and then Tim smiled, took hold of the bottle of scotch. and poured a shot into the tiny glass in front of Mark. "Ok, old man, here's your shot from this young man." He paused and then added, "I mean you're a customer and I'm just a bartender and as you would remember from your old days, the customer is always right. Right?"

Mark remained silent; his eyes fixed on the shot glass as Tim took the bottle away. Tim grinned slightly as he straightened up and gazed at Mark. Tim then reached for the glass, pulled it towards him, and poured it back into the dark bottle on the edge of the bar. Without looking at Tim, Mark said, "You may be a young kid, but I'm an old man. So, buzz off." Tim's smile faded away as he stared at the older man, who had an air of mystery about him. He had never seen him before, yet he had been sitting at the bar for hours, sipping on some port beer and watching TV. Tim wondered why he got so pissed off at him in a second. 'Oh well', he thought, 'something's bugging him', he wondered as he turned and left the bar area, heading across towards the kitchen.

Mark watched him disappear into the kitchen and then looked up as Manchester United scored a goal and the camera panned over the cheering fans. He straightened up, got off his stool, and walked towards the Men's Room. When Mark returned, the bar was still empty, and even Tim was nowhere to be seen. Mark looked up at the score, which was tied. He glanced around the bar, admiring the comfortable-looking tables and chairs and the cozy bar stools. He then rubbed his face and called out, "Barkeep, I need to pay my tab."

"He'll be back in a minute," a voice came from behind him, over against the wall where there was minimal lighting. Mark couldn't see anyone where the voice came from.

"Am I hearing a ghost?"

A guttural laugh came out from the dark area, "No, mister, just a man sitting down here minding his own..." he stuttered, then said "his own business, my man". It was quiet for a second and then the voice said, "The barkeep asked me to tell anyone that was looking for him that he would be back in a minute...minute or two."

Mark replied, "Am I drunk or what, buddy. Where are you and who are you?"

A laugh, then out of the darkness from the back part of the bar Mark could make out a tall, black man with a goatee, short, cropped hair, wide chest but a narrow build. As he slowly walked toward Mark, he saw that the man was dressed in Levi's and a black sweatshirt with a hood flopped on his neck. He came up to where Mark was sitting. He stopped a few feet away as a wide smile came across his face and he said, "I'm right here, partner, and the…the name's Magnificent… Magnificent Brown."

Mark was a bit intimidated by this big, black man, who came literally out of the darkness and stuttered a bit. For a split second, Mark thought he was having a mental breakdown and this image looming in front of him was some omen of life or death to come. He didn't respond and Magnificent just kept looking at him with a wide grin across his broad face. Finally, Mark said, "Magnificent, eh, now that is a great moniker. Me, I'm just a Mark."

"Well, just-A-Mark, are you leaving this joint or…or sticking around?"

Mark didn't respond as he just kept staring at this being looking right at him. He straightened up, smiled, and said, "Well, Mr. Magnificent, if I may call you that, my plans may have changed, assuming our missing Tim reappears."

"He'll be back shortly, my…my man."

"Well than, Mr. Magnificent, what's your life all about?"

Magnificent smiled, walked closer to Mark and sat down in the stool next to him. He turned towards him and said, "Living."

Mark abruptly laughed and said, "That, without a doubt, is the best response a person can give to that stupid question I asked."

Magnificent replied immediately, "No, I disagree. It was a good question. A legitimate one, especially in this day…day and age."

Mark said. "Whew, wow, I got a feeling I have a philosopher who can tell me what the hell I should do with the rest of the little time I have left."

Magnificent's smile spread slowly across his face.

CHAPTER NINE

The two men, one white and over seventy and the other, black, somewhere in his early thirties, just looked at each other, with frozen, blank expressions on their respective broad faces. The bar was dead silent except for the soccer match on the TV still going on in London. Two men, who had never met each other before, sat staring, stunned, at one another. Each was apparently waiting for the other to say something. Finally, Mark reached out with his right hand and said, "Mr. Magnificent, Mr. Mark here."

The black man's face stayed stolid. He looked at the hand pointed at him from an older, well-built white dude who looked to him like he had been around the world a few times. Slowly he reached out and clasped the large, white hand, something he hadn't done in quite a while. They both slowly pulled their hands away and just looked at each other as the TV announcer was yelling about a great goal for Manchester United.

"A goal," muttered Mark as his eyes went up to

the screen. "Like soccer, Mr. Magnificent?"

"No, football; defense, that's me. Pitt, linebacker, two years…you?"

"Baseball, first base, WVU… but I'd say about forty plus years before you played for the Panthers."

Magnificent smiled and slowly replied, "Forty plus, eh," his voice calm without any stuttering.

Mark replied, "Before you were born, probably," he paused and said, "Wow, you're in great shape."

"Just living in moderation, my man, moderation, meaning zilch. In fact, moderation in everything I do now, except one thing."

Mark smiled and replied, "And that is?"

"Friendship, my man, friendship."

They looked at each other, both with identical expressions of curious interest and wonder. Suddenly they both spoke at once.

Mark said "friendship," while Magnificent said "someone," simultaneously, and they both burst out laughing. Finally, Mark said, "Nothing personal, but I gotta have a dark beer with you, Mr. Magnificent. Something tells me that you are one different dude, if you know what I mean."

Magnificent straightened up with a huge grind, teeth bared, eyes wide open and replied, "Two dark ones, no pun intended, if they still have a no alcohol one for me."

As they looked at each other Tim reappeared down the bar waving a ticket in the air shouting at them, "I hit the lotto, I think."

Mark and Magnificent looked over at him in unison. Magnificent said, "How much?"

"I think a hundred bucks, if I'm reading this right," Tim replied.

"Wow, you can retire now, man," Magnificent replied, smiling.

"Hardly, but what the heck, a hundred bucks is a hundred bucks," Tim replied. "Least I can do is buy my only customers in this dead-as-a-doorknob bar a drink. Whadda you want, a shot or a refill?"

"Doornail," Magnificent replied.

Tim looked at him quizzically and replied, "Don't carry that brand. Guiness or Smithwick's is my best, I think…" he said pausing and then smiled, looking right at Magnificent and added, "Doorknob or doornail, now I get it. What the hell, you want a beer or not?"

Mark who had just watched this interaction piped up, "Either word probably works if you check out a dictionary, but to answer your question, lay a Smithwick's on me, as it looks like my quiet afternoon alone, wallowing over my shortened life expectancy has been beat by drinking beer with my newfound buddy by the name of Magnificent." He paused and added, "Much better than moaning and groaning around in my messed up brain. So lay it on me, barkeep and by the way, sorry for my crappy reply before."

Tim looked at him and replied, "No problem. I get worse than that in this joint," he replied as he turned to Mag and said, "So big guy what do you want?"

Magnificent replied, "Ain't got no money, no job, no life, no woman, no nothing, except a free beer, so lay it on me. At least I can look at it…unless you got an alcohol free one, my man."

"Got one, I think, my man," Tim responded with

a smile, as he stood looking at these two dissimilar men who seemed to have hit it off.

The three men stood in a triangle formation, all appearing equally taken aback by this sudden brotherhood formed of the common themes of their lives. Two of them had already briefly shared their current life situations. Tim, who was neutral, watched as the two men seemed momentarily unsure and quiet, looking at each other without speaking, while he looked back and forth between them. After a moment of silence, Tim spoke up and said, "Wow, I might have to pour a shot of Glenfiddich in the middle for the older guy, since the younger guy doesn't drink hard liquor. Hang on to your lives, guys, while I pour a couple, including one for myself." Then, he turned and walked over to the taps. Meanwhile, Mark and Magnificent continued to stare at each other from their seats. The two men were both apparently at a crossroads in their respective lives- one older white man and one younger black man.

Finally, the older man said to the younger, "You know, Magnificent, my whole life has been about bringing two parties together to settle disputes. Now I am trying to figure out how I am going to handle a life-threatening medical situation of my own but can't seem to figure out how I'm going to settle it for myself. I was about to squander my afternoon here by myself as I sat here sulking over my dilemma when out of the darkness comes this stranger who for some reason seems to be a man with a similar mindset. It's sort of weird that I think I figured you out pretty good in a minute or two, which means to me that you were supposed to pop out of the darkness of this old bar. Don't know why, but

I sense that you were supposed to come over to me. Maybe because you might be able to help me solve my dilemma."

Magnificent straightened up and a soft smile broke across his wide dark face exposing his white teeth, like a dual beacon of understanding as he responded, "I feel like a buddha of sorts because I sense I have known you for centuries. I feel like we battled together in a war somewhere and that we have come back together to figure out what our next existences are going to be. Me, solve your dilemma, my Man, maybe so. Hope so, then you can work on me," as he smiled and added, "As someone said, 'Let me show you the ways.'"

As they looked at each other Tim walked up and said, "Okay, here you go, guys," as he set down a shot in front of Mark and kept one in his hand. "This will get us started," as he tossed down a shot, put down the glass and went back to get the draft beers he had poured. In a few seconds he was back in front of them, setting down the mugs. Mark downed his shot, but Magnificent picked up his draft, looked at it and slid it toward Mark who noticed what he had done.

"No booze in that draft, my man," Tim said as he slid it from Mark back to Magnificent. Magnificent picked it up and took a sip. "Not bad, not bad at all. Good taste, such a reminder of my bygone—thank God—days."

It was quiet at the bar, only the soccer game announcers could be heard and then Mark said, "Give you credit, young man for stopping the booze. That takes real control. More power to you," as he paused and then leaned over and said to Magnificent, "As the oldest dude in this newly formed trio of life, I would like to start the meeting of the wise by predicting that when we part ways our lives will begin again anew and stronger."

Magnificent smiled and answered, "I'm with you, brother."

Tim seemed puzzled and said, "You're leaving already? I thought we were just getting started?"

"Well, not physically, but in a sense, we may be, and I have a feeling that when this bar starts to fill up with the usual crowds, it will get too loud and too busy for the three of us to talk anymore, so let's just set up a plan so that we can have another meeting of our minds soon," Mark stopped and looked at Magnificent and then to Tim and added, "By the way thanks for the drinks."

Magnificent sat up straight and said, "Thinking' about what you said, old man, and yeah, we should do it again. Something tells me this is good stuff. Okay, so now how do we start this round-robin of three?" he said to Mark and Tim.

Mark quickly replied, "How about five-minute stories of where we are right now in our lives. Maybe a minute or two of history and then the rest about where we think we are going or what we want to do with the rest of our lives." As he finished, he realized that he was settling into his mediation mode, naturally taking a leadership role the way, he did in his career.

Magnificent glanced at him and then across at Tim who had a puzzled look on his face. "Ground rules, good," as he paused and said, "you know I'm never one to be surprised or stunned by situations that come out of nowhere, but I'll tell you, Mark and you too, Tim,

I feel like I'm in the middle of one of the old mind-blowing movies when the world is about to explode and our own country is in total despair. The plot involves maybe three lives of quasi-ordinary people who don't know each other. Oh, I know you Tim, from the one other time I was here, oh, about a month ago, when I was destitute and came in with five bucks and you gave me lunch on the house and a coke which was all I could afford. Something I never forgot. A white dude bar-guy giving a desperate black dude lunch without a question. Never forgot that Tim, never will. Then here I come into the same place again with nothing, hoping maybe you could hit me again, 'cause I haven't eaten much except a bit at the "Y." Then wow, I meet some guru from nowhere who I believe I have known for centuries. He be white and I be black, and yet we've been together somewhere, sometime, I know that. And now we going to form a pact to figure out for each of us where the hell we are going with the life we have…. or something like that…" Magnificent pauses briefly, before saying, "make any sense?"

Tim was standing looking at the two of them and said, "I'm just a simple barkeep and listening to you two dudes feels like we're in the "Twilight Zone. When I was a little kid, I'd sit with my dad when he watched replays all the time of, oh shit, what was that guy's name?"

"Rod Serling," said Mark, quickly. "Used to watch that guy in black and white. Wow, and what an imagination. We need some of old Rod in this screwed up society."

"Yeah, Rod Serling. My Dad believed in all that

stuff and…" Tim paused and said, "maybe you two are heading into the Twilight Zone for real."

Magnificent piped up, "This place you have here, my man, maybe it is the Twilight Zone."

CHAPTER TEN

Magnificent met the only woman he had ever loved, when he was in his last year of his six year term in the Air Force after graduating from Pitt. She was a white woman from Manhattan and the daughter of a TV producer who was a millionaire. They met in New York when he was on leave from his military service. At that time, he had achieved one of his childhood dreams of flying a plane when a pilot let him sit in his seat while they flew supplies to a base in North Carolina. His other dream was to be on a TV show, and he spent hours watching shows in his grandma's living room. Being a black kid never bothered him because he always believed he could do whatever he set out to do. After finishing college at Pitt and while serving in the Air Force, Mag was stationed at McGuire Air Force Base in New Jersey during his last year of service. He would often go to New York City to experience the excitement of the city and try to see TV shows. One afternoon, about a week before he would be discharged, while trying on a sport coat at Macy's, a woman asked him if he had ever been in a play or any type of theater presentation. He was stunned and nervous when he looked at the beautiful, red-haired, white woman who was only a few inches shorter than him.

He had been nervous, and stuttered, "Ca..ca..can't say that I have. That was the beginning of the first and last female relationship Magnificent had ever had in his young life that was serious. It went on for three years and four months, after he was discharged, and it was the most glorious time of his life. Victoria McCallister, the woman who he met in Macy's was a child and woman of the most elite segment of America, that had ruled the country since its birth. Victoria worked as a scout for the broadcast executives, finding actors for TV and Broadway shows. She was a tall, willowy woman who initially was seriously enthralled by this well-built, black skinned man who had the exact specifications called for in an upcoming role for a partner of a well-known American actor who had starred in various TV programs. The lead actor needed a sidekick, who was big, preferably black, to appear with him in a serious cop drama based in New York. Who better than a vet; a cheap, unknown man, who was extremely eye-catching, and whom she knew would be attractive to women all over the U.S. What really set her off was that he would stutter once in a while, which she made sure was part of his odd, tough looking, but funny character. It didn't bother Magnificent because he had learned how to control the stutter, and could do it when he wanted to which worked out well as part of his character. She found him trying on a coat and in six weeks, he was cast as Deacon Don Downer on 'EVIDENCE,' a show that lasted three years until William, "Billy" Bailey, died of an overdose one night in his apartment overlooking the Hudson River. The show had to be cancelled and thus ended the career of Magnificent. His relationship with Vickie died with Billy Bailey and she moved on to new TV ventures as easily as changing the channel. Magnificent, who'd had no agent up until now, hired one, but after a year had passed without landing any roles, he found a job driving for a trucking company between Pittsburgh and anywhere, USA. He was traumatized by Vickie dumping him and began to drink whenever possible. Within two years, he had become an alcoholic and had lost his driving job. He then returned to Pittsburgh and did odd jobs. He lived in a room four blocks from where he grew up. By that time, his mother had died, only his sister and grandmother, at age ninety, were still alive. Even in his desperate life condition, both helped him as much as they could. Then one day, just weeks ago, he walked to a school that he had gone to as a kid many years ago on the North Side of Pittsburgh to get some food. He hadn't eaten for a couple days because the "Y" where he slept, had a fire and was closed. The gym of the school building he went to that day, had been turned into a food service for indigent folks in that part of town. He stood in line for close to an hour but finally got to the food counter.

After his filled his plate, Magnificent sat by himself in the corner of what had been a gym in the school's old days. The large, beamed room still had basketball backboards up against the ceiling. It was bustling with a large, mismatch of people; some in line waiting for their food handout and the others behind tables set up like a counter against the wall, doling out mash potatoes and green beans with apple sauce. He went back twice for re-fills and the second time, as he pushed his segmented, metal tray along the tabletops, someone spoke to him. He looked across to the server side and there was a tall, light-skinned, broad woman, with bundled, bleached blonde hair, dark blue eyes, probably in her fifties, smiling at him. He knew his face was spattered with gravy, and he had unshaved hair, and a frown on his face, as he looked over at her smiling at him.

"You, hungry, young man?" the woman, probably in her fifties, asked him as he walked past the metal containers filled with hot food. He knew from one look into her eyes, sunk deep into her well-traveled face, that she was a woman who had seen it all. After she plopped more mash potatoes and apple sauce onto his plate, she smiled and motioned for him to follow her. As he reached the end of the line she was standing there with that same wide, genuine smile and waved him to follow her to a different part of the gym. She went and sat down at a card table up against the glass brick wall with light shining brightly through from outside. She pushed paper cups off the table into a waste basket and pointed to him to sit down, which he promptly did. She sat down across from him, holding a large paper cup. She looked at him and said, "Go ahead, finish your meal, young man. Can't waste food or time, for that matter." Magnificent would never forget the look in her deep blue eyes and as he put a fork full of mash potatoes into his mouth with his eyes focused on her, he saw an ancient smile slowly expand across her fully lined face and she said to him. "Okay, buster, tell me your story."

For the next hours he talked to this strange woman. Most people had left the gym with only a few still sitting at card tables eating food and talking, laughing, and always looking around, as if someone was going to bust in and cut off the peacefulness of their meal. For some reason, Magnificent couldn't help but talk slowly and quietly to her. He only stuttered a bit as he talked about what he was going through at this stage in his life. Finally stopped and said to her, "By the way, what is your name…and why did you asked me to tell you my life story…?"

She sat up and said, "I didn't ask you to tell me your life story, you just started to ramble and eventually you told me something that is really fascinating and true, I'm sure. Oh, and my name is Veronica, V for short."

He gave her a stern look and said, "V…what's your story?"

She smiled, her face cracking in lines and replied, "You'll get it when you're done because I've heard a lot and am quite impressed by who you could be, Magnificent. I think you slipped in somewhere between page fifty and sixty of your biography, in this chapter."

This last line caused him to smile, an expression he hadn't felt on his face in months, maybe years. For some reason, this was the most relaxed he'd been in a very long time. He gave her his stolid look and said, "Okay, haven't had a home for a while,

or a place to stay for longer than a week or so, for months. I guess you could say I'm homeless."

She looked at him as if she had found her long-lost son; an expression of longing that lingered on her face. Finally, she said, "Not now, sonny boy, not now. Maybe your home now and don't even know it yet."

Magnificent's usual frozen face finally thawed a bit as another slight smile came to his wide brown face and he replied, "You know lady, for some reason, I feel I've met you somewhere along the way. You gotta whole name to go with your demeanor?"

She replied immediately, "'Demeanor, wow, the man must be some kind of writer. I mean 'demeanor.' You remember the old saying, 'De meaner de are, de harder de fall?"

Magnificent finally laughed heartily, "Whew, who the hell are you lady; that was a great comeback line if I ever heard one…oh, yeah, okay V, you gotta whole name?"

She looked at him, a smile breaking across her wide, crinkled cheek face as she replied, quietly this time, "As I said, my first name is Veronica and middle one is Angela. I have a last name, Rosario, which I only use for evidence of life in this world. If you care to, you can call me Veronica or V, as I said before. It all depends on how long you've known me. V is now my only name for folks I want to be with."

Magnificent was back to his shuttered, serious expression, and replied, "Well, thanks…Veronica, glad I made the cut. Hopefully I can call you 'V,' soon," as he paused and said, "so okay now lay your story on me."

V slowly replied, "Long novel, dude, very long and I really only like short stories."

Magnificent replied, "Well, you might not think so, but I read quite a bit from old books at the 'Y.' The old dudes from a long time ago, because the new ones take up space with bullshit and those old guys cut to the chase, as people used to say."

V replied, "You know for a young…or I should say a younger man, you act or talk like someone out of a hundred years ago. You sure you aren't a sort of ghost of years gone by?"

Again, Magnificent returned to his big time laugh as he answered her, "You know, V, you nailed me, cause there are times when I think I'm walking in a time way beyond my real time."

"What's real time?" she asked.

"Birth to death time," Mag repeated.

"Lifetime," V replied.

"Birth to death time is what I call it," Mag said again.

"What's that got to do with why you come off to me as living a hundred years ago?" V asked quietly.

Magnificent straightened up, turned, and looked at the now empty gym. All of the hungry, mixed bunch of people who were eating their meals before had gone, and the place was desolate. He looked back at the older woman who now looked to him like someone herself out of the distant past. 'Am I in a time warp?' he thought, looking at her worn face. He said, "For some reason it's the roaring twenties just before the depression and I'm trying to stay alive, cause I turned to booze over thought. I turned to hiding over facing reality. I got a hunch what's going to happen in the next hundred years, but I have no clue what's going to happen to me in this time zone."

It was dead quiet in the old gymnasium. V did not respond to his declaration. She reached into a dress pocket and pulled out two chocolate cookies she'd taken from the lunch counter. As she then looked up at Mag who was staring at her she began circling them around with her finger in the quiet. Then she looked over at him and said, "Know something, old sport… remember Gatsby," she said to him. "Oh, you wouldn't know him, but he was my man of a time long time ago. Gatsby waited and waited and was still searching for the love of his life and yet, he never got her. So, you are searching not for the love of your life, but just for your life, so let's you and me, find it together after getting to know each other for a couple hours. Whadda ya think, old sport?" she said as she pushed a cookie towards Mag and put one in her mouth.

CHAPTER ELEVEN

As Magnificent now sat across from the white man he had never met before he came into this bar, he smiled and thought back to V, the woman he also had never met before who he had spent hours talking to about his life just days ago. Two odd, different, but almost mythical people, who had just entered into his life. He sensed something in this life had started to happen for him. Something magnificent, a thought which made him smile.

Mark, the man across from him had a deep, serious look across his face and he interrupted Magnificent's digression of thought, "I see you got a full pint in your hand."

He responded, "Any pint you see in front of me, will be minus the booze. Don't get me wrong, I love this stuff, but don't drink it…no more."

Mark's expression slowly softened from his usually closed and stoic countenance to one of a gentle empathy expression. He immediately understood this man whom he had just met. He looked away from Magnificent and over to Tim who was standing behind the bar and said quietly, "I think you can take the beer and booze and fix me up with a coffee, if you got it, and whatever Magnificent here would like," he said pointing to Magnificent. "I think we need a table and in fact, you got any soup or anything like that, I think we both could use some?"

Tim came over to them and leaned over, "Got some chili that my wife made just this morning. Fact I got a huge pot of it left, because no one asked for any during lunch time." He turned and looked at Magnificent and said, "You want some, Magnificent?"

Magnificent smile and replied quickly, "About a barrel would do?"

Mark got off his seat at the bar and walked down to a triangular shaped booth at the corner where the back wall meets the side wall and sat down. Magnificent came and sat down across from him on the bench like seats. They sat silent for close to a minute without either moving. Finally, Mark broke the ice and said, "Okay, let's make a deal, what say?"

"Deal me in, new buddy," was Magnificent's quick reply.

Mark smiled and said, "I'm Mark and I'm dying."

Magnificent, sitting straight up across from Mark didn't reply, just kept looking at him. Then he said, "You got me beat, Mark, for sure. Think I'm going to be around for a while if I eat now and then, yet one never knows on this screwed up merry-go-round."

Tim came around then with two bowls of steaming chili, putting them down in front of Mark and Magnificent.

"You want bread? Got some really good dark bread."

"Lay it on me, Tim," said Magnificent, pausing as he added, "and sign me up to washing dishes to cover this plate."

Mark responded, "Don't worry, got it covered," as he watched Magnificent tear into the chili, breaking off a piece of bread almost simultaneously. "Man, you must be starved."

Slurping a bit, Magnificent said, "Thanks my man. Haven't eaten this good for, Christ, a couple days, I'm sure."

Mark's face twisted as he gazed upon the man before him. He could tell that this man had received extensive education due to his eloquence and intelligence no matter how he was dressed and apparently in a bad state. Mark couldn't help but wonder how this man had ended up in such a dire situation. The man hadn't eaten much in days, while Mark had a vast fortune of over 15 million dollars in Switzerland and maybe only months to live. As he watched the man devour the chili, Mark's mind froze as he contemplated the stranger's sudden appearance in his life. He couldn't help but think that the man was sent to him as a messenger from an unknown source during the most difficult time in his life. Mark snapped back to reality as the sounds of the man slurping and scraping the bowl brought him back to the present. He couldn't help but think that this could be a movie. "Whew, what am I doing here, for Christ's sake," he murmured to himself, then added "For someone's sake, anyway."

Magnificent looked up from his empty bowl at the chili Mark hadn't touched, and asked, "You gonna eat that, Mark?" Looking up at Mark then, he suddenly asked, "You, okay, my man?"

Mark pushed the bowl of chili across to Magnificent and said, "Eat up…And 'okay' is the right word." He paused as he looked across the table and said, "Last week my doctor told me I have probably an incurable situation that will probably kill me in months," he paused, took a sip of beer and added," but I could go through some shitty life-prolonging surgical procedures that might, key word is might, give me a couple more months, maybe a year of life." He paused, looking back towards the once-empty bar, now with two young men sitting there, and he looked back across to Magnificent, adding, "I don't want to go through that shit, man. No way."

Magnificent who'd been emptying Mark's bowl of chili, stopped in mid-air with a bite and then, with a look unusual for him, a look of sadness. He said quietly, "Well, my man, looks like we got some talking to do." He paused, then added, "You know when I came in this joint today, I was broke, hungry and dying for some quiet, peaceful time without worrying if I was ever going to find my self. For some reason, talking to you, as little as we have, for some reason, I think finding you is finding me. Know what I mean?"

Mark smiled slightly at the deep man across from him and said, "For some reason, I too sense talking to you might give me a clue what I'm going to do with what's left of this phenomenal life I've had. It's weird man, really weird." He said with the first broad smile circling his face.

Magnificent looked at Mark and a smile curled

onto his face. He pushed the filled beer mug away from him, straightened up his well framed body and said slowly, "I think we gonna get to know each other, brother, really well. Why, I do not know, but I got a feeling there was a reason why I walked into this joint this afternoon, starving and hungry, but I think more for a reason to exist than for food to stay alive."

Mark replied, "I have worked for over sixty years, non-stop, since I was a kid carrying golf bags for rich men. Worked at all kinds of jobs while in high school and college, then non-stop since getting out of the service," as he paused, "you want some more of me?"

Magnificent waved his hand and said, "Yeah, man, go on."

"Well, I had a solid childhood. Only child of two parents who worked. My dad worked for the railroad and was gone all the time and my mom, she taught in junior high. Small town on the Mon, you know, Monongahela," as he looked at a stoic Magnificent who was looking at him directly in the eyes and he continued. "We lived by the river next to railroad tracks that in those days were busy all of the time. Trains ricocheting by and horns tooting all the time. Mom made every meal for us all those days. Only other kids in the family were her sister's kids, who we saw a lot of during the holidays. I guess it was a typical household for those days." He stopped and looked over at Magnificent who for the first time since they had been talking, looked bored. "What I miss?" he said.

"Typical white folks, I get it. Okay, go ahead," Magnificent slowly said.

Mark took a sip of his coffee and said, "Yeh,

you're right there, but you know, young man, and you are young by my standards, for some weird reason, I get the feeling that you and me are kindred spirits," he paused and added, "You know Magnificent, I think in these really down days for me, my man, as you would kindly say, this meeting of ours was meant to be. Never been a religious man, but I am a believer in some kind of spirit that secretly, quietly like some radio beam, flows through this atmosphere of ours generated by something, some power that can unify, or prevent, human connections. You know what I'm saying?"

Magnificent's face softened and he replied, "I do, my man, I do. You know I've been in some shitty relationships in my life, from my in-and-out father to my soft and generous mother, who sacrificed as much as she could to keep me alive. Then I had a white woman for a couple of years, the only one I've ever had and that fell through. That started my downhill run until I just met an older lady a few days ago who I think may help me turn my life around. Yet, you know, even though I know now what I got to do, when I came into this joint today, I did not have a clue, as to the what and the where of my life; what I needed to do and how I was going to do it. Know what I mean?"

Mark quickly responded, "I do, because for the past week, I have had, for the first time in my life, not a clue what I was going to do with what's left of this life of mine," as he paused, then said, "In my life, I have accomplished so much, all on my own; my way, and I've helped many lives in the process just by showing them solutions to problems they could not handle. And here I was, with no clue as to how to solve my own life crisis."

Magnificent replied, "Well, let's work on that, whadda ya say?"

Mark replied, "You know Mag, if I can shorten your name, I have worked all over this world since I was, oh, twenty-five. I interviewed an old guy from Philly who had a business of bringing people and companies together, who was a bit older than I am now and ill. I interviewed him and he hired me. You may not believe this, but my first job for him was to go to Sweden and talk to a company that wanted to buy a steel company in Pittsburgh, which was part of the reason he hired me. He sent me to Stockholm to talk to them. He just needed contact made, not necessarily for me to solve the problem. My God, I was twenty-five."

Magnificent kept looking at Mark, no reaction to what he was saying. Then he said, "Okay, so what did you do?"

"I went. Pittsburgh to New York to London to Stockholm. The two guys were at the airport in a limo after a guy with a sign was standing for passengers entering the airport lobby with my name on it in big red letters. Me, I was duded up in a brown suit, raincoat, hat over my forehead, making me look maybe thirty, and shaking like a leaf in the wind. Oh, I smiled, as fake as I could come up with, and got into the back seat next to a guy who looked like a Nazi war criminal even though I knew he was Swedish. No smile, just a tight handshake and a "Hallow, I'm Lars Johannson." As I dropped into the seat, the guy in the front seat next to the driver said, "Peter Olson. We're going to a place down the street for openers. Mark, right?"

I stuttered to him, "Right." I was scared shitless, as

we drove through a dark, rainy afternoon in downtown Stockholm, until we pulled alongside a wood and stone building, which I assumed was the restaurant which it was. We were in the restaurant for two hours; they each had two drinks and I passed, as they laid out how they needed to make a deal immediately to sew up the purchase of Three Rivers Steel, which was a combo of four smaller companies that had merged in the early seventies as production of steel had begun to slow down in the valleys of Pittsburgh. My boss had given me Three Rivers Steel acceptance contract if what these two guys offered worked. Well, it did. I explained what Three Rivers wanted to Lars and Peter who said yes right away, and the deal was done. You won't believe what happened that day, Mag. You won't believe it, but it was the beginning of my life's career. That in one day."

Magnificent smiled slowly and said, "As someone once said, 'It was meant to be', my man."

CHAPTER TWELVE

Mark glanced away from Mag and over at a group of young people who had taken over the bar, reminiscing about his own youth when he had just started his working career. He turned back to Mag who was watching him attentively, "You wanted hear more, Mr. Mag?"

"You got the floor, as they say in the U.S. Congress, I think," he replied with his wide smile spreading across his dark face.

"Okay, here goes." Mark described his job as like that of an umpire in baseball or a referee in football, where he called strikes and offsides. He explained how over the years his work expanded greatly due to his unique ability to talk to people who often disagreed and even hated each other. Mark stated how amazed he was that so many successful people and firms were so dogmatic and selfish about their financial achievements while not being willing to sacrifice a fraction of their wealth to keep what they had achieved. For some reason, he could quickly assess people and determine what might help them understand the reasoning of the person sitting across the table from them. He had such a quiet, persistent, reasonable, and sensible way of calming dissent and promoting positive compromise. By the age of thirty, he was a millionaire and owned apartments in New York, Stockholm, and Mt. Washington, overlooking Pittsburgh. He looked across at this man he had just met, paused, and asked, "Okay, so far so good?"

Mag slowly smiled, "Right on, my man," as he paused and added, "Is that it?" he asked.

"No way. I'm just getting started," as Mark paused and said, "Oh yeh, I'd found somehow, and magically, a career that for some reason found me and made me suddenly rich, but fortunately not famous. Mag, I never stopped, for anything. In ten years, I was thirty-five and had money in a bank in Switzerland, just gaining interest. I was alone. No wife, no kids, no nothing. Both of my parents, who I really didn't spend time with when I was younger, had died. No brothers, sisters, cousins, or anybody related to me that I knew of. There I was: a single, young man who this old man…" as he paused and laughed a quiet smirk and added, "actually a bit younger than I am now… who for some reason took a liking to me, this young guy from Pittsburgh that had quickly and honestly handled his first job, which was a very important project in Sweden for him because he could not have handled it because of his age and medical problems. Okay, now Mag, you'll like this part. This is the story of how this all started with an old guy about my age now, ironically. You ready?"

"Fire away, my man.

"Okay, this man, Homer McKibben, now in his

late sixties, had been in WW II as a paratrooper. At age thirty-nine, his last jump ended him in a Nazi prison where he was rescued in December when the Allied troops pushed into Germany. What a guy. He stayed in Germany when the war was over and began to talk to companies, mostly German and some in Switzerland who were trying to recoup and recover. Some were unique and had survived the war but needed both manpower and equity which Homer found in the U.S., England and even Australia. Within ten years, Homer, who called his company International Equities, a name I think he invented, became a quiet, effective mechanism for raising capital and creating mergers all over the burgeoning world of the 1950's and 1960's. So, within twenty years he was a millionaire, about ten times over, living in Philadelphia and Zurich, and found himself with all this money, securities, a deceased wife, and two children, both girls. As got into his seventies, medical problems threatened him, and he began looking for someone who could help him handle his thriving business. His medical problems would not allow him to travel as he had done all his life. In those pre-internet days, as I said, I found him through a friend from my military days who had met him by helping him get information on a possible project in Philadelphia. Homer mentioned to Dudley Downer, my acquaintance from my military years, that he was looking for a young person to help him at this stage of his life who was trustworthy, but hardworking. Dudley worked for a major New York investor, and he thought of me." Mark paused and said to an entranced Mag, who seemed spellbound by his tale, "Whew, sorry, got carried away.

Mag waved a hand at him and said, "Mark, my man, you should write a book about this history you got. It's a hell of a story, for sure. No go ahead, you got me, especially about the old trooper."

"Well, that's how it all started. So, I went to Philly; met Homer; spent about a week with him and after that time, he said to me, 'Son, I don't know why or how, but you remind me of me when I was your age.' I remember clearly saying to him, 'Homer, I could never have jumped for the first time in a parachute over France with bullets being fired at me at any age, but at 39, wow, you are something'. I remember adding this clearly as if I had said it yesterday, 'Then after the war to have the guts to approach those companies in Europe and help them become flourishing international companies. You are a miracle man.' I can still see this gray haired, now slightly built man wipe tears from his eyes, and saying to me, 'Thank you so much'. Thank me so much, Jesus Christ, the guy made me what I am today," as Mark paused with a tearful looking face and bent his head down towards a static, slightly smiling Mag who was slowly shaking his head.

"What have I walked into this day?" Mag said quietly, as he reached across the table of the booth and patted the hand of this man who had literally come out of nowhere into his life. The loud noises of chatter and dishes clanking filled the bar, but they were easily able to talk over them.

Mark replied, "A life, my life. But you know when I'm done, you're going to give me your excuse for being here. I got a hunch we may have a lot in common." As he straightened up there was a ting. "Christ, only a couple people have my number, and it hasn't rung much all week, thank God. Sorry, Mag, let me take this."

Magnificent waved at Mark who opened his black phone and said quietly, "Hello." He listened for a few seconds and replied, "Okay, I'll get back to you but not until tomorrow. I'm in a critical conversation right now." He listened and then replied, "I know nothing is more critical than what you have to tell me, I get it. But give me 'til," he looked at his watch and added, "Nine am, tomorrow." He listened and snapped shut the phone and turned to Magnificent. "Just my doctor," he said as he looked across the table. "Okay, where were we?"

Mag smiled and replied, "Not we, you."

CHAPTER THIRTEEN

Mark had lived an eventful life for over five decades, filled with work and travel that provided him with incredible experiences and income. However, everything had changed in an instant when he received his medical analysis. With no family or close friends, Mark was a highly successful broker who brought people and organizations together, even when they didn't want to cooperate. Although his work gave him personal gratification, his millions of dollars provided little personal peace as he processed his medical dilemma. Mark had traveled all over the world during his military career and his work life to places he had only read about as a child. During his military service, he spent most of his time in Washington, D.C., except for his early days at Fort Knox, Kentucky. However, in his last year, he was sent to several exciting places around the world to visit new computer sites in military bases. His military training and work allowed him to mingle with the military and corporate elite who were developing early computer technology systems to defend and later create attack systems. The highlight of his last year was traveling around the world and experiencing ancient cultures in different countries, which enchanted him.

Mark had a strong desire to explore the world and see the places he had only read about. After compiling more money than he ever could imagine having, he satisfied his new founded desire of spending time in places he had always read about. So, he began to buy condos in strategically located areas that he could visit while working. When he began, he relied on phones and fax machines to communicate and copy contracts. But as technology advanced, he began using computers, cell phones, and iPads for all his business and personal interests. Mark would sometimes travel from remote areas with low populations to bustling cities with millions of people. He would work for hours non-stop on his computer, then pause to enjoy the view from a window or porch, often with a glass of his favorite Porter dark beer. Mark had a minimal social life, having been in only three relationships with women over the years, the last one lasting almost ten years. He could have married any of them, but he was never ready to commit to another person's life. Mark was completely devoted to his work, not for the money, but for the satisfaction of bringing people together to find solutions to their problems. Mark had a fear of hurting others, which he could not understand, which he wondered off and on, if this was why he could never commit to the women he did have great affection for. He often felt inadequate when he met people with great relationships and families. This fear may have been genetic, as both his parents described their own parents as strict, solitary, and cruel people. Despite his personal struggles, Mark was content with the fact that he was only responsible for his own life and could not harm others.

Mark understood the introspective nature of his parents after they talked about how difficult it was raising a son. Their focus on their own internal struggles helped Mark understand why he had a solitary existence. Mark valued life as a unique creation, recognizing that the human brain allows for quick decision-making that impacts one's life. He appreciated his parents for providing him with the freedom to live his life as he saw fit. Looking back, Mark respected how his parents maintained their independence and respect for each other despite their separate personal needs. His father, a veterinarian who loved to hunt and fish, spent his free time in his Allegheny River cabin near Brady Bend, PA. Meanwhile, Mark's mother worked as a librarian at the Carnegie Museum in Oakland after years at their hometown library in Monongahela.

In her later years, his mother was also a yoga teacher, who spent weekends at sites around Pittsburgh and traveled on her vacation time, by herself, all over the country to visit meditation events and even traveled twice across the Pacific to Tibet. With all this individualism in their relationship, they maintained a quiet, gentle respect for each other, and they understood each other's needs for solitary pursuit of their passions. Mark, their only child, became so independent throughout his schooling days, that by the time he graduated from high school with straight A's, as captain of the school tennis team, Mark had been pretty much on his own. They had paid for his college tuition at West Virginia University where his mother had gone. He'd done extremely well and graduated in three years while playing tennis and working during summer vacations at a travel agency. No fraternity life for him, just studying, receiving high honors, graduating, and then entering the service which was required of men in those days. He had always wanted to spend time in the service, which for some reason had always fascinated him. His parents divorced while he was at college, and he rarely saw either one of them in his military and working years. Ironically, they died apart, yet in the same year, twenty years ago. His dad drowned when ice broke in the Allegheny River during a horrific winter and his mother six months later in her sleep from probably a heart valve that somehow clogged; both were in their eighties. They both had lived solo after their divorce, yet both had lived vital lives devoted to their own needs, beliefs, and values. An odd couple for sure, with few friends and no familial relationships on either side; just a few cousins that Mark had never met.

For sure, it was an odd and unusual family situation, but one which he appreciated. Yet, deep down now, as he faced possibly his own demise, he had been depressed the last few days, and he knew a large part of it stemmed from the fact that that he was in his later years and faced with the probability of losing his life soon with no family at all. Yesterday he had calculated that his net worth was close to twenty million dollars, ninety percent of it salted away in Switzerland, the balance in his local Pittsburgh bank. Mark had spent weeks at a time in Zurich as he grew to love the beautiful city in the mountains where he had a chalet outside of the town center. Recently he had become upset about what he would do with that wealth that he had worked so hard to create. Somehow his ability, his life work, that helped people understand that solutions were better than conflict when their individual financial existence depended on it, was now in jeopardy. Learning last week of his potential death had been the most difficult situation he had ever encountered in his regimented, programmed and fulfilling life and he would have no negotiator helping him, it was him alone.

Mark's thoughts then drifted to his past relationship with Mary Martha McGuire, a woman he had dated and remained friendly with despite their on-and-off status. Mary was an accomplished author and Rhodes Scholar who had written biographies of successful women in male-dominated fields. Mark had always found it easy to talk to her, even after they stopped seeing each other. The last time they'd spoken was almost a decade ago. The day last week when Mark had learned he had a serious medical condition, he'd spent that day and night drinking heavily, which was uncharacteristic for him. The next morning, he called Mary on a whim and was surprised when she answered. They talked for almost an hour, and Mark felt closer to her than he had in a long time. He confided in her about his medical situation, something he rarely did with anyone. Mary was sympathetic and positive, assuring him that there had been a lot of recent medical advancements made in the field of cancer treatments and advancements that could help him beat his form of cancer. She'd encouraged him to try them. Mark was grateful for her support and her positive attitude, which lifted his spirits. He had always thought he could handle his problems alone, but talking to Mary had made him realize that sometimes it was okay to lean on others. Before ending the call, she invited him to her family's old and spacious beach house in Maine. He expressed his gratitude and promised to consider the offer. Since their conversation, he couldn't stop thinking about the kind and attractive person who had encouraged him to persevere through his struggles.

Slowly Mark's thoughts returned to where he was, and he looked across at his new black friend who was standing up at the bar talking to a young man. He must have realized Mark was looking at him because he turned and waved. Mag gave a friendly tap to the shoulder of the guy he'd been talking with and proceeded toward Mark's booth.

Mark had to wonder if Mag had been sent by a higher power to help him through his difficult time. As the muscular black man sat down and gave him a penetrating gaze, Mark couldn't help but ponder who this mysterious figure could be. Mark said, "Mag, you're still here?"

Mag's composed face didn't shift as he replied, "Ain't going nowhere my man. I'll say this again. I'm just mesmerized by us sitting here as if some force had brought us together." Then he paused and added, "Actually, while you were staring over at me and probably going over your situation in your head, my mind exploded into 'what the hell am I going to do when I leave this joint?' I came in here, starving. Now I'm full. I came in here not sure where I was going to sleep tonight and hoping the Y is re-opened and yet, I now have no fear of that or anything. What have you given me, white man?"

he paused and added, "You know something else white man, I haven't stuttered at all since I started talking to you. Now what the hell does that mean?"

Mark smiled and replied slowly, "I'm no doctor for sure, but I would say that maybe you're mentally relaxed and secure when you're talking with me, which makes me feel good. Something like that." He paused for a second, then said, "Just now you mentioned your stuttering and asked what I had given you. That you're not fearful anymore about things that have been bothering you. Let me turn that around, Mag. Given you?", Mark said pointedly, as he paused and went on, "I was thinking the opposite, cause, I think you've given me courage and an idea of what I should do next in what's left of this phenomenal life I've had." Mark paused, looked right at Mag, and said calmly, "How would you like, oh I don't know, four or five, maybe more, million dollars, my man?"

Magnificent, without cracking a smile, slowly reached out and patted Mark's right hand as he said, "Five, or no deal."

Mark broke out in a fit of laughter as he leaned over to grab Magnificent's hand and shake it. Meeting his eyes, Mark said, "It's a deal. The 'Fixer' has struck again," he said with a rare smile on his face.

Magnificent looked at him and replied, "The Fixer? Who the hell are you anyway? The Mob, CIA; who the hell are you?"

Mark patted their hands and pulled his hand away and said, "Well, I used to be known as "The Fixer" in my line of work. Not CIA or the Mob, just me. I had a knack for bringing people together when they thought they had no way to do so. So, I was called ""The Fixer" because I could bring them together to mutually solve a problem that seemed unfixable, thus "The Fixer". And as "The Fixer", I got paid very well. So well, that I have quite a nice account across the waves."

"Man, you are something else. I can't believe I just walked in off the street to get a cup of soup or something and I meet you, the "Fixer Man.""

"'Fixer Man,' I love it," Mark responded with a smile, as he looked across the table at this man who had been dropped into his life by providence.

They were both quiet for a few seconds as the noise from the bar picked up which was now filled with young folks; boys, girls, and apparently a couple of in-betweeners, who were either sitting or standing along the bar. None paid any attention to the old white guy and the younger black guy who were sitting at the booth against the plaster faced booth against the wall.

Mag broke their silence and said, "Well, Fixer Man, when do I get my five mil, now or after you have another coffee or are you going back to beer?"

Mark's calm face now turned tight as he replied, "I'm sticking with coffee and I hope you're kidding, Mag, because did you think I was serious? Give some guy who I don't know, some guy who stopped drinking, I assume because he was so messed up, he couldn't function anymore. Who just sits across from me for a couple of hours and then assumes I, who have worked my ass off for close to fifty years, am going to just turn over five million dollars to him. Are you serious or just jazzing me?"

Mag quickly replied, "Love jazz, man. It's my

music, not yours, and yeah, I am serious. I could do a lot with five mil, a whole lot."

"This conversation which has been literally out of this world has now become of this screwed up world. Why should I give you five big ones?"

Without hesitation, Mag replied, "So I can do some good in this screwed up world."

Mark straightened up and answered quickly, "'Enough, said, my Man, enough said. I was thinking about a Porter beer, but I'm sticking to coffee. I'll see if our boy Tim has any coffee because you and me are going to have some deep-thinking talk."

Mag smiled slightly and replied, "Deep thinking. Whew, we've come a long way, in a short time," as Tim approached their table.

"You guys are having a ball. Thank God Denise came in to help, 'cause I was about to ask you two to pitch in. You need anything?" Tim asked.

"Perfect timing, barkeep. You got any fresh coffee back there. We're going to need some because we have some heavy-duty talking to do," Mark replied.

"Just made some for myself," Tim smiled and turned back to the bar. "Be right back, guys."

"Okay, where were we, Mag. Oh, yeah, we're going talk about that blunder of mine in laying 5 million on you."

"Blunder," Mag answered. "Thought we had a deal. Had it all spent, just thinking and kidding, my man."

Mark looked over at Mag and said, "Son, and you are a son, compared to this old sod, I was serious. Life is too short for some and too long for others. I think, based on our little talk today, that for us, it's too short and especially for me. So, let's just talk about what you and I want to accomplish with this time we have left on this earth; what say?"

"Hold it for a while. I gotta take a leak. Be right back," he said looking across at Mark, then scurrying towards the bar and to the Men's Room.

Mark watched him go as Tim brought a coffee container with cups and saucers on a wooden tray.

"Where's the big guy?" he said as he put the tray on the table.

"Off to the Men's Room which I'll probably have to do myself pretty soon, but what the hell, I'll take that fresh java. I got some thinking to do."

CHAPTER FOURTEEN

Mark sat sipping his coffee at the back table where he was thinking about the life changing experiences with a man literally out of the universe. He began reflecting on the events of the day and the past week. He realized that this time was the most important in a life that had been full of ups and downs. His philosophy on life was being challenged. Over the years, Mark had developed his own view of what life really was. He believed it was a moment that had been created by millions of years of evolution, starting from a single cell, and eventually developing into humans. Now, faced with the end of his existence, he was rethinking his beliefs. He understood that all species are created and pursue a life before passing on to somewhere or nowhere. Mark had always believed in the latter, but now his belief was being put to the test. He wondered if this was some sort of plan written specifically for him, as he mentally reconstructed his understanding of humanity's purpose on Earth.

Mark's mind wandered to a man he hadn't thought

of in years, but whose beliefs seemed relevant to his current situation. About twenty years ago, while strolling up a San Francisco hill that reminded him of Pittsburgh, he encountered a young man, speaking quietly to himself on a bench. Intrigued, Mark stopped and listened to him talk about his belief in what life represents, is how he put it. He listened for a few minutes and then sat down beside the young man and spoke with him for at least an hour. When Mark tried to give him a couple hundred-dollar bills, the young man refused. So, Mark asked for his full name, address, phone numbers and email address which had just become part of our society. Mark stayed in touch with the young man, Oliver, over the ensuing years, and his story and beliefs had a tremendous impact on Mark's life. In talking and emailing him he found out about his life and beliefs.

Oliver McGill was a man from Portland, Maine, who traveled the world and lived his life according to his own needs, both personal and humane. He often used the term "humanely" to describe human life and its similarities and differences from other species on Earth. He taught Mark about the essence of life, which Mark never forgot and tried to incorporate in his life. However, last year, Mark read on Oliver's Facebook page an entry by someone that he had died suddenly in Alaska at the age of fifty-five, where he had recently moved to. Mark was shocked as he thought Oliver was only in his early twenties when they met. He contacted Oliver's sister, Sandra McGill Brown, who he had talked to him about when they were together. He told her about his meeting with her brother. Sandra informed Mark that Oliver was a loner but an intelligent being who remembered every detail of his life since he was a child. He had written poetry and short plays throughout his life and had a few long relationships, but never married. Sandra had found a small notebook with Mark's name in it and asked if she could send it to him. Mark was thrilled to receive it and discovered many small poems in Haiku style, which Oliver had written to illustrate his observations on life within just seventeen syllables. Oliver was cremated in Alaska, and Mark cherished the notebook as a reminder of their meeting.

Strangely in the ensuing years from meeting Oliver and talking for hours with him, Mark began to write haiku type three-line poems in a pocket notebook based on his observations of life. It was the beginning of his own self-learned belief in the unlimited existence within the Universe. Mark began to believe there was no beginning or end of the Universe; it just existed, and humanity was simply a creative result of the it's collaborating elements. Where those creative elements came from, was to him the mystery. His mind at this time in his life was probably like it was as a teenager when he struggled with what he was going to do with his life. It was then that he began to write out weekly plans for what he had to do. Plans for how he was to live and succeed in his life. From that time on, he always had a plan, whether that was where he was going to eat or where he was going to go next. His success ratio was so great in his career that his reputation as a closer became universal. Now at this time in his life, he faced the ultimate closer situation: his life's end. He had no clue what he was going to do in the short time he had left. He reached into his back pocket and pulled out his battered, leather notebook and opened it up to a clean page. He pulled out the small, lead pencil he kept in the notebook. As he looked at the blank page, he glanced at the last poem he had written. He smiled, remembering that he had been sitting in an airport watching a black lady pushing a cart with her luggage stacked on it. As she got to the revolving door, she waited patiently for it to come around and then pushed her cart into the door opening. A tall, skinny white guy with a beard stopped the door from moving so she could enter. She turned, smiled, and gave him a thumb's up as the door began to move again, with her in it. The guy returned the thumbs up with his own. Mark looked at his notebook and read what he had written about what he had seen. "Lovely dark lady, overwhelmed with her baggage; White guy helps!" Mark smiled, realizing it was a lousy haiku, but at least he had noticed the man's action and gave him credit for his kindness. 'Oh, if the world of humans acted that way all of the time', he thought, then remembered clearly that he had also thought, 'In most cases they do'. It was just the small percentage of usually egotistical, self-indulgent men or women who only cared about themselves that could give humanity a bad name. Mark had lived and worked with this element of people over the span of his career, usually the ones at either end of the table when he was settling issues that they hadn't wanted to be solved because it made them look weak. The 'made them look weak' thought, caused him to smile and he tapped the table with his right-hand fist as he thought went on, 'My God, humanity, with the middle of that word being man, can be so controlled by so few people'. Just thinking about Oliver made his mind work overtime as he processed his thoughts.

Mark continued thinking about Oliver and his self-centered but peaceful life. As far as Mark knew, Oliver had never hurt anyone. Oliver believed that life had absolute significance, and humans often substituted adjectives like "glad" and "blessed" for human existence. Mark had adopted Oliver's beliefs over the years and believed that humans had a brief moment to exist in the unending essence of the Universe. The Universe had always existed and would never end, and it was a vacuum entity within which stars, planets, black holes, and other structures, elements, and beings existed and interacted with each other. Mark believed that Oliver must have come from another source of being other than Earth and was of the Universe. This belief made Mark realize that each person must travel their own road of destiny in the most personal way possible. Mark had been a loner in his life but ironically brought certain extroverted humans together and settled their disputes. He had saved his earnings for proper use later in life. However, he was now concerned about the proper use of all his wealth since he faced the possibility of his life ending soon. Regardless of Oliver's influence, Mark had to resolve this personal situation of his wealth hidden away in Switzerland's mountains.

As his mind drifted away from his old, unique friend Oliver, it switched his thoughts to Mark to his new friend Mag who had disappeared. He looked to the end of the bar and then saw Mag talking to two men. Mark wished he could have introduced Mag to his old friend Oliver, as they would have hit it off. He smiled at the thought that maybe Oliver had somehow returned to him through Mag. Looking back at the bar, Mark saw Mag still talking to the men. Mag must have felt Mark looking at him because he turned, saw him and waved at him, as if they were old friends, and continued talking to the men.

Mark's thoughts returned to his current life situation and what the hell he was going to do. He was now scheduled to go tomorrow morning to see Dr. Whitaker and Dr. Wisnewski, who were going to set up a plan for him to try and stop the spread of his cancer. For the first time in years, he didn't want to go to a meeting. His normal life was shaped around meetings and bringing people together. But this meeting was for hearing how these two doctors planned to halt the spread of the cancer on his prostrate. The first couple days he had read extensively about cancer in that area of one's body and it was not encouraging; the odds were against him living longer than six months. There were possibilities; new treatments coming and a new surgical procedure, which Dr. Wisnewski mentioned just before their meeting ended. One of these possibilities might be the right solution for his situation. The cancer was apparently in a location that made it possible for some of the new treatments to have a positive effect on the cells. He looked at the clock over the bar. It was almost four. He'd been here for almost five hours. He had come in by himself and now had become attached to a homeless guy. Mag was at that very moment wending his way towards him.

"I'm back, partner," came Mag, sliding into the seat across from him. "Where were we?"

Mark smiled softly as he looked across at this

man who had entered his life from out of nowhere to become someone important to him so quickly. "Quite a session I laid on you, but it gave me time to float all over the place as I wondered, what am I doing here with some guy from out of nowhere who I'm professing all my previously unprofessed life secrets. Yet, it made me realize that maybe you represent what I have come to believe."

"And what the hell would that be?" Mag asked before pausing and smiling slightly and adding, "well, maybe I know what that might be."

"Let me tell you about a friend I knew years ago that got me thinking about the realities of this thing we call life. Maybe it will explain why we're hooking up today, okay?" Mark replied.

"Lay it on me, my man, I ain't flying anywhere today, " Mag replied, as he crossed his arms and sat back.

CHAPTER FIFTEEN

"About fifteen years ago I met a guy you would really like. As I thought of him when you were gone, a thought came to me that you remind me of him. You are a totally different in age, size, color, everything, but for some reason you get to me like he did."

"Tell me about my double," Mag replied.

"You may not like what I tell you," Mark responded.

"Let me decide about that," Mag countered.

"Okay, let me see…where or how should I start," Mark countered.

"You talk best when you just let it all hang out is what I've figured out in our short lifetime together," Mag replied.

"Funny you should use the word lifetime…because that is sort of what I was going to talk about, using my guy as…let me start something," Mark said slowly.

Mag straightened up and said, "Get on with it."

"Okay, this guy I met was as close to being a guru as I have ever met, yet he looked like some guy from

McKeesport and ironically, he was born up along the Allegheny River near Brady's Bend, if you know where that is. Anyway, he had short hair that was grayish-brown and a full head of it. His eyes were deep blue and large, and his body was straight and narrow, though I could tell that it was solid. He always had glasses around his neck on a cord, and whenever he needed to read something to support his ideas, he would pull up the glasses. As he read to me, he did it slowly, very slowly, and then he would pull down his glasses and explain in his own words what he had read. I look back on my times with Oliver McGill and realize that the man had a significant impact on my life. His way of living, especially in these days of the internet society, has made me understand and appreciate life better. Now, I want to share with you this new way of understanding and living our lives. It may interest you, who knows. However, it will take some time, my new friend. As I look at you, I believe you will understand both what I have come to believe and what Oliver McGill believed and lived, even after he passed away."

Mag said, "As I watched and listened to you, brother, I realized that you probably think when you're done, that I won't top your story, tale, or whatever you're gonna lay on me, with my novel of life, but mine might be an eye-opener."

Mark smiled and said, "It wouldn't surprise me a bit—in fact, I expect your story to amaze me, because I sense and have sensed, that you are an old soul who's lived many lifetimes."

Mag replied, "Man, you know me better than I know myself but down deep inside here," he said as he tapped his head, "I always knew I'd been somewhere a long time ago and I'm just back for more," he finished with that huge smile of his. Then he added, "Just kidding, man. Well sort of, I guess what I mean is that we all have millions of years of human connectivity flowing through our brains, in my opinion, and what you and me are doing right now is just pausing a bit. Make any sense?"

"Absolutely, Mag, absolutely. Couldn't have said it better, myself," said Mark.

"Oh, as you were talking, something came to me that I know fits in," Mag replied.

"What's that, Mag?" Mark asked.

"I have a lady who will fit right in with where I think we're going. She goes by Veronica, but I call her just V. She's closer to your age, come to think about it, and she found me wandering around in life days ago and she is the one who literally and immediately found something in me I never knew was there," Mag said.

"What was that, may I ask?" Mark asked.

"Life and me, in that order," Mag responded.

Mark looked at him with a serious look that tightened his face as he replied, "Yeah, I think I'd better meet this Veronica, because I think we're reaching out for literally the bottom line."

Mag replied, "I'm going to contact her, but first go on, I know your far from that bottom line."

"That I am and so, let's see…okay, well back to Oliver McGill. I knew him, actually spent many days with him, for, as I said, close to fifteen years. I'd always stop by to see him, once even in the Himalayas where he was living for quite a few years. But in the States, he'd always return, a small town in Maine by the ocean.

He loved quiet; he loved the beach, especially with strong, violent at times, waves. Oliver always lived what he called the "Nature Culture." That is how he lived. Water, whether it be a river or an ocean or rain or wind blowing. Water off a waterfall, somewhere deep in the middle of nowhere, which he would always find and return to, year after year; he was fascinated by water. Water, to him, was the power-personified of nature. When he came back here, he'd rent a cabin in a bend in the Allegheny River near where he was brought up. To him nature, that is the land, the oceans, the winds, the rivers, the animals; anything that was non-human, but pro-universe or closer to our existence, pro-nature. That was his life's blanket which covered him, twenty-four hours of every day of his life. I talked many times with him about this belief. Eventually, after months and years, I came to believe he had nailed our civilization and any other out there," as he paused and added, "Telling my story of Oliver to you Mag feels like I am passing on his virtues to someone who will accept and understand the man's unique and powerful philosophy."

For seconds it was quiet as Mark and Mag just looked at each other, then Mag said, "I would have liked to meet this dude. In some ways, though I'm from a different culture, black as black can be, educated in a sub-culture in my youth with prejudice a given, but brought up by proud, strong folks who were religious, which I'm not now. But that world was mine until I left my home and went to college, then the service. I realized one's destiny is only, key word only, achieved through individual effort. Oh, white folks grow up rich in their sound, segregated communities, college, jobs easy to get and family easy to create and life easy to live, but most folks, even poor white ones, struggle to exist at all. Now this is not new at all; that is the way humanity has always been, and in my opinion will always be," as he paused, took a deep breath and went on, "But. If one can somehow recognize the realities of their given and from somewhere deep inside their…their…can't think of the right word…I'll use 'constitution,' is a core fireball of singular strength that only they have. If they realize their strength of self, that it exists, then maybe they can grab something to be able to pursue a life of fulfillment. Maybe, then maybe, they can live a life that has internal meaning to them and they can not only live a positive, powerful life, but they can also bring others who suffer along with them," as Mag paused, and added, "that, my Man, is where I am, as I try to work my way out of this current time of negativity, of just physically surviving. Bottom line, I need to find an existence of living a life based on my singular, unique abilities that will allow me to live, literally. You know food, a place to come back to at night, and some peace and enjoyment in this existence we call humanity. And then also to pass on my positive existence to others seeking what I have achieved. That, my new friend, if I may call you that, is my life goal," as he paused again, and added, "Whew, where did that all come from?"

Again there was silence, then Mark reached across and took a hold of Mag's arm, squeezed it gently, and said, "My man, there is a power, a source that brought us together and also has taken a hold of your consciousness or whatever we want to call it and has just allowed you to perfectly express where you've been; what you have gone through; and where you will be going. I wish I would have gone through that tunnel of life many years ago, but now that I may be near the end, at least I am close to the other side before I do go elsewhere," as he paused and said, "And I know you and Oliver have crisscrossed with that same source that brought us together."

Mag smiled his slow, crinkled smile and replied, "I sensed we have met based on your description of the man and as far as you're concerned, you're prepared to face the situation you're in. The game ain't over yet. You may have another quarter left. A lot can happen in the final minutes of play. Maybe you'll connect on a long pass in the endzone, my man. Big Ben threw a couple when it looked like it was all over."

Mark chuckled and said, "So he did, and I was there. February 1st, 2009, when he threw that incredible pass to Santonio Holmes with 35 seconds to play in the corner of the endzone. I was blown away and wow, just thinking about it makes me tingle," as he paused and wiped tears from his eyes and added, "Well, maybe Mag, you nailed it or me. Guess I'll have to go tomorrow to see my doc's and see if I can find my receiver in the end zone," which caused him to smile again and say, "End zone. Pretty appropriate wouldn't you say?"

"Well, it could also be time for a kick-off to keep the game going," Mag responded.

Tim walked up with a plate covered with a paper towel with steam coming out and put it down on the table. "You guys must be starved. I hope you got the world's problems solved because looking up at CNN while my young dudes suck up beer and don't give a shit about the world coming to an end, I actually forgot you were over here in the dark. Cause, those folks haven't stopped drinking, laughing and putting up big tabs which is okay with me. So here, this will pick you up. Had some myself."

Mark looked at it and said, "What is that, if I may ask?"

Tim replied, "You may and it's chili con carne ala me."

Mag said, "Let me at it. Love that stuff."

Tim added, "Stuff it is. Now if you need anything else let me know. Gotta get back to the juvies."

Mark slid his watch down so he could see it and leaned over, looking at it closely, said, "Man, or I should say, Mag, I gotta get some sleep because I got that death knell of a meeting tomorrow with my doc's. Eat up."

"Hope it goes better than you think, 'cause you got a lot more to do, I got the feeling," Mag responded.

Mark picked up his raincoat from the seat beside him and put it on as he stood up. He looked down at Mag who was digging into the chili and said, "Mag, how about we get together late in the AM tomorrow morning. Right here, if that is ok?"

"That will work," he replied as he put his fork down.

Mark reached into his pants pocket and pulled out a wad of bills. He looked over at Mag and said, "Now, listen. I know you are a special guy and one not looking for handouts, but this is not a handout. It is only a loan because I know this time next year, wherever you are, you will have conquered any needs you have, so take this and go down the street to the Hilton and get a room."

Mag looked at him with a sullen face and said, "First, thanks, my man, much appreciated, but the Y is all fixed up now and has a great set up for me. One I can afford since it costs nothing."

Mark smiled and said, "Okay, but please take some of this dough, so you can eat right. I'd like to meet you here tomorrow after my meeting with the doc's because I have a feeling it will not be a good one."

CHAPTER SIXTEEN

’Where am I going with this life of mine?’, was Mark’s thinking as he took the elevator down from his doctor’s office.

He knew one thing, he was going to have them do the new procedure on him that might, ‘just might’, as Doctor Whitaker said several times, ‘beat this son-of-a-bitch’. Checking his watch, he walked briskly out of the blue and white building that housed the offices of a slew of doctors working for the university hospital system. It was a mecca for state-of-the-art life-saving new methodologies in health care. Mark has always been proud of his hometown Pittsburgh becoming a worldwide hub for experimental healthcare ever since the day Dr. Thomas Starzl arrived and began his kidney and liver transplant services that changed transplantation in the world and saved many lives. Now that medical procedures were in place with the likes of Drs. Whitaker and Wisnewski creating new methods of handling pancreatic cancer, Mark realized it just might give him some extra lifetime. He smiled a bit with that possibility as he picked up his walk down Fifth Avenue, heading for a coffee shop to just sit and think for a while.

As he had listened to Drs. Whitaker and Wisnewski talk about this experimental surgery that 'just might' save or at least extend his life, Mark's mind had wandered all over the place. Here he was, a lone man with no family, extremely wealthy, who just might die alone, with no one to care about him. His mind, always actively thinking, was churning with thoughts of why he had no one in this world. No one, meaning no other close friend or family member that he connected deeply with, though he knew and worked with many people.

"Café latte, please," he told the young, blonde girl behind the counter." He slowly walked over amidst an array of young people, probably all going to college at Pitt. Mark felt years older than his actual age as he looked at the clothing the young ones wore in the coffee shop, as if they all had gone to Goodwill and grabbed stuff out of boxes, except each bit of cloth probably cost hundreds of dollars. Jeans slit above the knees that probably cost three hundred bucks. He smiled as he stood waiting for his latte.

The place was alive with sounds as these young folks went about their lives. 'Noise seems to legitimize their lives' he thought to himself. He, certainly of the old school, cherished quiet. He remembered when he would be in one of his critical meetings with oligarchs or corporate big shots, he always made sure he was between them. He would put his hands up at any surrounding noise, whether it was music on hidden loudspeakers, or a window open to loud traffic outside, to ward it off. When they looked at him questioningly, he would quietly say, "Noise pisses me off." Without an exception, they would look at each other and then back to him in between them, but would stay quiet, probably for the first time in months. He announced, when they were seated, that he arranged, that their three-way meetings were to be held in strict silence except his own voice or the responses of the opposing sides. These were the only sounds in the room that he allowed. Problems were solved, he swore, in half the time as when people were surrounded by noise. He forbade their associates, cell phones and laptops at the meetings. He allowed yellow, legal-sized notepads only. They could jot down their notes and refer to them, but that was it. When a contract was signed, of course, there was an associate allowed to join them, but they weren't allowed to speak; just read and finalize the contract. Noise was just not acceptable in Mark's mediation meetings.

Of course, traveling and connecting with contacts, whether in buildings or airports, noise was prevalent, but in making important decisions, noise wasn't allowed in his life. It was an effective strategy, and now, as he stood waiting for his latte, he smiled, as the noise factor was overwhelming. Fortunately, his latte was put on the counter, and he put down a ten spot, picked it up, smiled at the barista in thanks, and went over to a corner table to sit and process all that had happened to him this morning and go over his incredible time he had with his rare new friend. He'd already spent more time yesterday with Mag than he had with anyone else in years, except in a professional capacity. He took a deep breath and looked out on to the busy sidewalk as a bevy of students of all sizes, colors, and dress; boys, girls, and crossovers, as he called those of switched sex, based on what some reporter he heard call folks in between. Also, their hair had all colors possible, no matter their gender. 'What a difficult life these days are for young people,' he thought. Then he realized that these days were all these young ones knew and that some of them would look back at these days and think the same thing he was about the youth when they got older.

Mark sipped his latte. Suddenly he was in a funk as he thought of their future days that he wouldn't know anything about. Then just as quickly, he smiled, as he thought of how different he had become since learning of and facing the idea of his eminent possible death. All these years, since leaving the service and years of his incredible success at playing the middleman for usually very well-to-do businesspeople, when he himself had come out of a middle-class background, he had never thought about his eventual and inevitable death. Life for him had always been the action of living, with no thought of its obvious end. Oh, there were times in his travels when flights were scary, but he never thought he would be affected. 'What a selfish, stupid bastard I have been', he thought.

Although surrounded by students and their laptops with a buzz flowing through the cafe, Mark suddenly felt like he was in a tomb. It was stiflingly quiet. His mind was stuck in a loop of thoughts that progressed from childhood; to women; then to an island off Sweden; and for some out of nowhere reason, Ella Fitzgerald, his favorite singer was wailing "Someone to Watch Over Me". Her powerful voice wove through his mental sound imagery, and in a flash, he was back in the Starbucks. He looked around, disconcerted. He felt somehow like a huge weight had been mysteriously lifted from him. For some reason, he now felt calm, more internally positive; and strangely, simply looking forward to his coming days. Why this mental trip, he did not understand. So, he picked up his latte and finished it as a broad smile crossed his face. Life might be different and shorter than we would choose sometimes, but he felt powerful, confident. He felt that he could live with this new limitation affecting his body, because his mind was still free and agile.

Mark lifted the coffee cup to his mouth, finished the coffee and slid his coffee cup over to the edge of the table into a waste container. Stretching his body, he stood up and headed for the front door, passing a line of students, phones in hand, necks down and tapping going on. He smiled at this new world.

CHAPTER SEVENTEEN

Magnificent had spent the night in his tiny room at the Y, sleeping soundly for the first time in months. As he lay there awake, for the first time in a very long time, he felt at peace. Mark came into his thoughts, and he returned to their time together yesterday. He knew it was not luck, but something meant to happen. He also thought about Veronica or V, as she said he could call her, because he wanted to see her this morning before he met Mark at the bar, to see if he could coerce to come with him to meet Mark. For some reason he had a feeling she and Mark would hit it off, philosophically.

Mag believed that their beliefs would connect them, and they would understand each other perfectly. He wasn't completely sure, but he was determined to bring them together. However, he had to hurry before she started analyzing someone else. He had met her a few days ago at the food counter at the old school that was set up to help indigent people like himself. Ironically it was the grade school he had gone to when he was a kid. He was at his lowest point, and she had zeroed in on him, which literally pulled him out of his negative state. He quickly got dressed in his same clothes he'd worn for days and made his way down the stairs and out of the Y. Mag enjoyed walking nowadays as it helped him exercise his once-powerful body that had deteriorated over the past three years. He even used the machines at the Y every day.

All ages of people used the facility for breakfast; students and older people and lunches for anyone of any age. V made a point of especially providing care to high school age boys for breakfasts, who didn't receive much attention with difficult home situations. Young girls seemed to have more people helping them in their schooling, and in their lives, but boys often refused to get help, possibly due to machismo. As he walked to see her, Mag remembered all that had happened the day he first met V. She had told him that she spotted him in the food line and for some reason wanted to talk to him as to why big, younger man was in this line for food. When they were talking, despite him telling him he was called Mag, she always called him by his full name, Magnificent. When they talked that day, she told him that he made a strange impression on her when she saw him in the food line, with his dark skin, huge build, and thick facial hair. She said his glassy eyes startled her at first, but there was something about him that struck her immediately. But what got her, she had said, when he approached her in the food line that day, was that he broke into a great smile that warmed her heart. She remembered him saying, "I'm Magnificent, ma'am!"

and that she had replied with her own smile, 'You sure are, son, you sure are. What would you like today?" He remembered saying to her, for no reason, "A large bowl of your advice would do fine." He would never forget that she smiled and replied right away, "I'll be done here in a few minutes. Maybe I'll bring that bowl of advice for dessert", she had said and added, "Stick around, we can have a chat."

Now, he was back in the same room where he had met her, and she was serving some very young kids breakfast food. She looked up and saw him and waved for him to come over, which he did.

"You hungry?"

"No, I'm good. I'll just go over there in the corner, where I used to be in grade school," he said with a huge smile.

She waved him off and headed back to the kitchen area. Mag sat down at a table, leaning back against the light blue wall with paint peeling off. He looked across the dining area at the old clock with a black rim, surrounding a white face with hands at five minutes to eleven. It was the same clock that had been here when he went to school many years ago. He smiled as it reminded him of a clock that was in his grandma's kitchen for years; the second hand had never worked. He spotted Veronica coming around the end of the food line and heading towards him. An older, deep dark man, probably in his seventies, gently touched her arm as she passed. She stopped, and they talked. Veronica patted him on his shoulder, waved a goodbye and headed towards Mag.

"Who's your buddy?"

"Willie Crawford. Was a big-time fighter in his

time," she replied as she sat down across from Magnificent.

Mag smiled and replied, "That was Willie Crawford. Jesus, I read all about him when I was a kid."

"Yeah, he was something else. Fought Floyd Patterson. Almost beat him. Willie could punch and Floyd could box. He caught him once and nearly tore off his head, but Floyd was a dandy. He could dance with the best of them and jiggled around until he gained his brain back and finally finished the round. He won seven of ten rounds, Floyd did, but old Willie gave him a go."

She straightened up and said, "So, Magnificent, how you been and where you been?"

"Well, you know me. Just moving and grooving, but I'm doing good. No booze and I'm working out at the Y. The bod is getting in good shape. Other than that, nothing special. Oh, except some guy I need you to spend time with…I mean you, me, and him."

Veronica smiled, "What the hell is that supposed to mean?"

"It means for the first time in my life, I met a guy who is from this world, but maybe, Veronica, another one or soon to be there."

"What the hell does that mean?"

"It means he is a fascinating dude who I think you would connect with based on our talk of the other day. You really made a big-time impression on me, V, and after talking with my new old friend, I think you two would hit it off. He is of this world, but he talks like he is out of this world. Know what I mean?"

She looked at him and smiled slowly, "Coming from you and how you said it, I'd say I would, for some reason." She paused and added, "So why is so important to you, Magnificent?"

"For some reason, V, I got this urge for the three of us to meet up."

"You trying to fix me up, Mag?" she said with that smile of hers that always grabbed him.

He returned a slight smile, cheeks crinkling and said, "You could say that! Yeah, I am, but not for that stuff. I think we three have something in common."

"What's that, may I ask?"

"You may and my answer is we have a similar view, sense, make it belief of what life is all about."

"You got me now, Mag, for sure. When do we meet this messiah?"

Mag looked across at the old clock and he said, "Well, I know the hour hand in the old clock doesn't work, but I think he'll be in his pulpit by the time we get there."

"We going to a church?" she replied.

"Sort of," he said as he slid off the bench and stood up. "Can you leave soon?"

"Yep, my job for today is done. These little kids didn't have any breakfast and we had a lot left over, so they got a good breakfast for an early lunch. I'm not working lunch coming up, so it works out well for me to go with you to meet this guy."

"Okay, it's not too far a walk so we can walk over."

"Lead the way, Mag," Veronica said, as she straightened up and walked over to Magnificent.

CHAPTER EIGHTEEN

Mark walked into the bar well before noon and Tim was standing at the cash register putting bills into it. As if by some special power he seemed to know when Mark walked, he turned to wave with his one free hand. "Welcome back, old dude, you," he said as he turned back to the register. Without looking down at Mark he said, "I'm open, but it's early for anybody."

Mark went to the middle of the bar, which was empty of any customers. Even the TV was off as Mark continued working on the register. "I know this isn't a Starbucks, but can a paying customer get a coffee young man?" he said as he pulled out a bar chair and slid on to it.

Tim turned with a pencil in his mouth and smiled, then took out the pencil and said, "Early yes and coffee yes," as he paused, looked at Mark and said, "Back for another session, oh wise man of the world."

Mark, now sitting at the bar, replied, "Man, you were listening to Mag and me, weren't you?"

"You had me mesmerized, but I was so busy with the young crowd I didn't get all that you two were talking about, but I did notice that Mag, when I heard him, didn't stutter once."

Mark smiled and replied, "You know something, you're right. At first, he did a little when we were first talking. He would just nod his head, and I thought I caught a stutter, but after a while he was really into it and you're right, I can't remember him stuttering anymore."

"For him, that is something. The one other time he was n here, he only stayed for a short time, never drank anything, just drank a Coke, but when he did talk, he stuttered a bit and seemed to be self-conscious. I mean, he's such a big, husky dude who I would never want to anger and yet, his voice broke a couple times like a little kid. I felt sorry for him, but as you two went at it and I overheard you, he wasn't stuttering at all."

"Well, we got into quite a deep discussion about, well life in general, I guess you could say," Mark said quietly.

"That would keep anyone busy…oh, let me get you that coffee," Tim replied.

"Well, yes, a coffee first would be great. Got some thinking to do, Tim. Just came from a doctor's office and I'm either going to drink coffee all day or switch to some of that scotch up there."

"One of those doctor's visits, eh?", Tim responded.

"For sure, one of those. Actually, one of those you don't want to have," Mark added.

"Be right back. You staying there or do you want it in your private office over in the corner against the wall?" Tim asked.

Mark responded, "Good idea. Over there. Don't want any company today until I get my mind cleared up."

"How about if Magnificent shows up?" Tim asked.

"Over there, for sure", Mark replied as he stood up and walked over to the table in the booth against the wall. He turned and said to Tim, "He is something else Tim and I'm sure he'll be here. Hope so, anyway."

"Be right back with the java," Tim responded.

Mark rubbed his face with both hands and looked up at the blank TV screen. "Nothing there", he murmured and then smiled as he said, "'Nothing there when it's on, for that matter."

He straightened up in the chair, realizing that he felt tired. Last night he had tossed and turned for hours, which was unusual for him. As he sat there, he thought back to his session with the doctors. He remembered that he was so much on edge when he got to the doctor's office that when he was waiting to be called in, ironically, he had dozed off. He hadn't responded to Lou, Dr. Whitaker's nurse when she called him, and she'd had to come over and tapped him on his shoulder. She asked him if he was ready which got him out of his slumber. He had followed Lou into the offices of Dr. Whitaker slowly. It was unusual for him to walk into an office hesitantly. His whole life he had entered an office like it was his, but not this time. He would never forget that meeting.

"Grab a seat, Mark, Dr. Wisnewski will be here in a few minutes," Lou had told him quietly.

Mark remembered slowly walking over to a grey, curved leather-looking chair and sitting down. He sat there for just about a minute and Dr. Whitaker came in, shook Mark's hand, and went to his large, wide, old-fashioned wooden desk. He looked at the doctor who had a slight smile on his face as stood behind his large wooden desk.

Mark rubbed his forehead, straightened up and said, "Well, what's the verdict?"

Dr. Whitaker pulled his chair out and sat down. He looked across at Mark and said, "We'll wait for Dr. Wisnewski, as we do have a plan, but I want him here before we lay it out for you."

Mark had looked at him. Dr. Whitaker was a stern-faced middle-aged doctor with deep blue eyes, who rarely smiled. However, at times, a slight crinkle would appear at the corners of his eyes, usually based on a pun he made during a non-medical discussion. Mark recalled that the doctor had smiled that way only once, during their first meeting, when he had mentioned being single and having no known relatives. This brought that slight extension of the doctor's lips as he replied, "You are more of a loner than I realized, Mark."

Mark remembered his reply at the time, just as Dr. Wisnewski came into the office, "That I am doc, and now I am glad I have been."

Dr. Wisnewski came over and shook his hand and went back beside Dr. Whitakers desk. It was quiet for a few seconds and then he looked right at Mark and slowly discussed a new surgical procedure that both doctors believed to be promising. The procedure he told him about would utilize new data technology that would hopefully isolate the cancerous area more accurately than ever before, and they would then be able to extract it. If successful, the procedure could possibly extend his life by several years, maybe even longer, if it didn't reoccur. Only five patients had so far received this particular procedure that utilized technology only recently developed. Mark's chance of increased life expectancy was at about 20 percent, but Dr. Wisnewski outlined this surgery plan and described his chances of longer life as being very feasible, based on the narrow extensiveness of his cancer. Mark processed 'narrow extensiveness' for the next half hour and when it was stone quiet in the office, they asked what he thought he would like to do.

Mark cleared his throat and he strongly said to them, "I'll go with it, but I have a couple things to clear up, but I will get back to you in a day or two at the most. Thank you both and I do want to proceed." He then got up and walked up to Dr. Wisnewski, still standing and shook his hand. Then he walked over to Dr. Whitaker's who stood up and he shook his hand.

Dr. Whitaker replied, "We'll get things set up, Mark. Just call us as soon as you can in order to get a head start on processing the new procedure protocol".

Mark left the hospital and walked to a bench across the street and sat down. Quietly and with his feet crossed he watched people of all ages, colors, and dress walk by him. 'Wonder how they're all doing,' he remembered thinking.

CHAPTER NINETEEN

Tim walked over to the booth along the back wall of the bar with a small pot of coffee and a cup on a saucer. He put it down in front of Mark and said, "Well, here's some fresh brewed black stuff. It'll pick you up."

Mark smiled, "You know, son, if I may call you that, been thinking just now about our session yesterday and it was the most provocative, positive time I have ever had, believe me."

Tim smiled, "Oh, I do. I could tell. Your session lasted through my quiet time, my awful, noisy time, and my quiet nighttime. I could not believe you guys could sit there and bullshit your way through a whole day. Very impressive….and you're back, yet."

"I sure am, and I may need a boost later," as he picked up the small pot and poured himself a coffee. Tim put down the pot and went back to the bar as several young student types came in and sat down at the bar. Mark sipped his coffee and his head dropped as his mind had him wondering what the hell was going on inside him. For the first time in so long he felt alone, like he was in it all by himself. He smiled as he said to himself, 'this thing we call life.'

As if by some intuition, as he sat, head bent, suddenly he felt someone was looking down at him and he slowly looked up into the still, slightly smiling face of Magnificent, and beside him a wide-faced middle-aged woman with a serious look in her eyes, who was staring right at him. Instantly, he felt a regeneration fire through his mind as he saw Mag and the woman looking at him. He straightened up and replied with vigor from somewhere, "Well, here we are again, Mag, and I see the lady you talked about, I do believe."

"You do, Mark." Mag turned toward Veronica and said, "May I introduce you to my other new friend, Veronica Angela or V, as she prefers."

Mark got up and reached out to V to clasp her hand with both of his and said, "V, so nice to meet you. Mag has talked much about you and I'm glad he brought you by to our cozy, little corner."

V smiled and replied, "Could become a critical corner for us all, Mark. Magnificent talked so highly of your…belief system that I wanted to share it."

V and Mag sat down at the wooden table as Mark waved at Tim, who was looking at them from behind the bar. He waved and gave back a one-minute sign with a finger as he returned to what he was doing at the bar. For a few seconds the three just sat quietly until V said, "So, Mark, how are things this day?"

"Funny…this is a day I never thought I would be contemplating in this life of mine."

V responded, "Contemplation of life. Wow, that is

quite the way for us to begin our…relationship brought to us by this man, Magnificent." She paused a second and added, "And actually he and I have initiated our own interesting and positive relationship which I hope you and I can duplicate."

"Whoa," Mark replied, "you are way ahead of me. I haven't even laid out my …situation," he paused looked away from her towards the bar, then back to her broad, serious, but soft, lovely face and added, "of having an operation that I hope will take care of my prostate situation which maybe Mag may have told you about V, if I may call you that?"

V replied, "You may, Mark, you may."

Mag tapped the table and said, "May I interject?" Mark and V both sort of nodded in unison as Mag noted and then said, "Your doctor's decision, right? An operation?"

"Right," Mark replied.

Mag said, "Okay, can you tell me..us, about it?"

Mark straightened up and said quietly, "Well, it's a new procedure that thankfully is one that deals with the location and type of cancer that I seem to have. It's potentially a life saver…at least for a few years depending on the cancer that's being eliminated doesn't reoccur."

Mag replied, "Well, hell, my man, that's terrific. You know when it's going to be done?"

Mark responded, "It's up to me, but probably in the next few days. I just have to call them, and they will set it up."

V said, "Let me tell you something, Mark. A good friend of mine had a similar procedure done last year, but it was on her intestine, and they got all the cancer.

So far there hasn't been any reoccurrence."

Mark smiled slightly, "Well that's good news and hopefully they'll get it all from me and I can get on with my life."

Mag tapped Mark's arm and said, "My man, I'll...,' paused looked at V, who smiled at him, "...we'll be with you. So, I'd say, go for it."

Mark responded, "Thanks. That means a lot to me because as strange as this may sound, I was thinking about how I really haven't got anybody in my life," as he paused looked away and then back to Mag and V saying, "It's so funny, but my coming in here yesterday and meeting you, Mag and now V, has to have been set up by some force out there." He paused for a few seconds and added," Wow, you know you have calmed me down, Mag and you too V, thanks for your presence."

It was quiet at the table as the three seemed affected by what they all had said concerning this difficult situation they had just entered. Then the quiet was interrupted by the arrival of Tim who said a little too enthusiastically for the solemn tone of their discussion, "Okay, you all, what can I get you?"

V spoke up first and said, "You know, I got a feeling this is going to be quite a day for me. Why, I'm not sure, but get me a double shot of Glenlivet, if you have it."

Mag looked at her a bit shocked, and Mark smiled as Tim replied, "Coming up, mam and you Mag, a Sprite or something like that?"

Mag paused and replied, "Yeah, Sprite is fine. I'll let my lady friend do my drinking."

Tim asked, "Mark, more coffee?"

"No, my friends here have put me in a much better mood, so lay a Porter on me, Tim," Mark responded.

"Okay, will do. Be right back," Tim replied and left.

They sat quiet again before Mark straightened up and said, "What the hell, as someone said, 'You only go around once'," as he paused then said, "You know, as V said, for some unknown reason she had a feeling that this is going to be quite a day. Funny, I feel the same way and it brought a thought to me which came after what Mag and I went through yesterday. Each day can be a life. Why, I don't have a clue, but for some reason, I think each of our days can in themselves be your life. Or, based on my medical situation, one should live each day as if it is your life."

V looked at him, a smile crinkled her face and she said, "Mark that was so profound. I know I just met you and Mag days ago, but, wow, I think that could be a theme for this discussion or at least the beginning, and maybe the end, of what we come up with. Each day is a life. Wow I like it."

Mark replied, "You know, that does sort of sum up how I feel at this moment. This day may be my life, or at least how I end up living it. A day is a life; wow, I'm getting prophetic in my current state."

Mag smiled and said, "Had a hunch that you two would see eye-to-eye, at least looking at each other in that way. And…I think after a while, in many phases of what I think we'll be delving into. So, let's just see what happens."

"Well, for me, I'm calmer that I have someone, or two, to whom I can vomit out my dilemma," Mark said with a slight smile.

V smiled, "That's one way to put it, I must say," as Tim came by with a small glass of dark scotch for her, a glass of Sprite for Mag and a mug filled with very dark beer for Mark. "Well," she said, as she picked up her glass. "Here's to us guys, if I may use that expression. May we listen to each other and change the world for everybody else."

Mark picked up his mug of dark brown ale; V had her glass already up in front of her and Mag was pouring his Sprite. Mag lifted his glass, and they all clinked their glasses together in a silent toast before drinking.

Mark lowered his glass down a bit and said, "What is this going to bring?"

CHAPTER TWENTY

It was dark in their space across from the bar, which was beginning to fill up with customers, mostly students, there for drinks and the lunch specials made by Tim's wife. In their corner booth, Mark, Mag and V, had talked endlessly about their beliefs or understandings about life from their own perspective. Then at times one of them would raise their hand like in school, when they had questions about the various topics. It was a quiet, sustained discussion which lasted for hours, only pausing when sandwiches were brought, and another round of beverages were ordered and delivered.

At one point, V said to Mag, "what have you got me into my fine friend. I cannot believe I am spending this day with one old guy and one young guy, both expressing life in a way I have never considered, yet in ways that tie in with my own beliefs."

Mark smiled and said, "Lady V, you are a genius, if I have ever met one."

V smiled and replied, "Based on everything you've

told us, Mark, I feel like you are a solo in a large chorus of people. From what you've said, you've never been married; left your home, which apparently was a substantial one, and never looked or literally went back; do not seem to need others, even though your whole adult life you have brought angry, awful people together and made them find unity when they literally, in most cases, hated the other party. I find your life so intriguing and so very unique. You, seemingly, have never been dependent on any other human which is a characteristic I have never come across before in my years of life and in helping others,"

Mag interjected, "Right on, sister, right on. But I say let's sort of put together our manifesto. Let me do something if you all don't mind."

Mark shot back, "Shoot, my man."

V responded, "Can't wait."

Mag straightened up and said, "Okay, then. Here's how I see it or would like to see it…" he paused, looking out at the bar, took a deep breath, and turned back to his two cohorts at the table. Mag said, "Okay, first. The first time I talked to this dude sitting across from me, and of course I mean Mark, I stuttered a bit. It was noticeable to me…it was to me anyway, but I eventually held it back. I have stuttered since I was very young, especially when I was nervous about something. You'll notice, folks, that I haven't once stuttered, and you know why?" He paused expectantly before finishing, "Because for the first time in my life, when I met you Mark and then you, a lady, that I began to truly believe I began to find myself. For some weird reason, I 've never been this confident about living my life before. The essence of this is a sense, a positive belief you two have helped create for me in just our brief times together. It's also got me thinking about the vastness of this universe and how we are just three humans who have somehow come together as if some mysterious power made it happen," as he paused and said, "You know what's funny, is who would have thought that I said what I just said, because I'm just a nigger from the slums and you all are white folk from the suburbs," as he paused again and added with a slight smile, "but that I said it and I know you will accept what I said because it is so important to me," as he paused again and continued, "Wow, sorry, had to say that." It was quiet for a few seconds and Mag added, "One more thing. Listening to you two and adding my own thoughts, I think we are on to something really important. But what really hit me, was listening to you two within a few days; an entrepreneur and a caregiver, expressing to me what you both believe in about human life, and you did not know each other, is too ironic for it to be just chance. I think it was meant to be and that you told these beliefs to me, is more than ironic."

It was silent for a few seconds, then Mark said, "A veteran, huh, you were," Mark injected with a smile. "Wow, I want to re-enlist."

"Me too," V responded. "Where have you been all these years, my fine friend and by the way I didn't grow up in the suburbs and my dad was a brown dude from Cleveland. My Mom was a white babe from the suburbs and Scottish."

Mag replied, "I didn't know, but you two still discovered me."

Mark interjected, "I do have a comment, though,

about what we have been discussing. We all have watched programs, read books, heard scientists talk about the universe, and listening to your dissertation, Mag, I have one element I need to add: It's possible that there are many minor universes, like ours, present in the never ending, never beginning macro-Universe. It just keeps regenerating; possibly dying and being reborn or just simply born continually anew. We don't know, do we. We will never know, probably. But, man, as they gained internal intelligence, has always wanted a place to go after death; better known by religion as heaven. If one dies believing they're going to heaven, of course, it makes their last moments more enjoyable or comfortable or whatever, so we invented that comfort. What we have discussed is that our life is simply a human life no different than an animal life. We are born; we live; and we die. So, let's make that middle one as fulfilling as possible."

V smiled and said, "That is it, my friends, that is it."

It was quiet for the first time in hours. No back and forth. No voices raised, just silence. Mag stretched his large body; Mark twisted his back and finished his beer; and V sat up and knocked down a shot of Glenlivet.

At the same time, all three began to speak, which caused, for the first-time, uproarious laughter from this so-serious threesome. Backs bent and smiles spread, as they all quieted.

Finally, Mark said, with a chuckle. "Well, gang of three, now that we have human life settled, I guess we should see if we can get a show on the Science Channel." He paused and added, "But seriously, how are we going to put this together into a simple philosophy for first ourselves, and secondly, for exploring the possibility of spreading our belief to folks seeking an understanding of what human life is really about? We know the beginning, sperm city; and we know life itself, up and down existence; and most importantly, we know the end result; I call it peace," as he paused and added, "You know, something else I've been thinking about is maybe in this, I think positive life of ours, we can find some way to make life more fulfilling for some folks who've never had a chance to do so. Know what I mean?", he asked.

V looked at Mark and said, "Wow, I like that one. It ties right in with our philosophy. We can have our belief of the universe, but we can also put our beliefs to work in this existence of ours by helping those who don't have a chance. I see It every day," she paused and said, "Something for this trio to think about, I'd say." We can work on our philosophy why we also work on the reality of this existence on this planet. A great combo, I'd say."

Mag said, "Those two beliefs are potent. Right on, you two. That's a mantra for us, for sure."

"Let's get on with it," Mark roared.

CHAPTER TWENTY-ONE

For the first time in hours, it was quiet at the back corner table, which must have made Tim realize that his longest lasting customers were probably needing either drink or food, or both. He came over to a now quiet trio, just sitting, looking intently at each other. He tapped on the table.

"Guys, it's me, the owner. Remember me?"

All three suddenly looked up at him. Mark responded, "Wow, Tim, we have been really crisscrossing our philosophies and I think we're sort of mesmerized by all that we have said..." he paused and said, "but yes, we remember you and yes, I think we need some food to replenish ourselves. It's been quite a session, at least for me."

"Got any good burgers?" V asked, looking up at Mark.

"Oh, with cheddar, if you have it...oh, and tomatoes."

"Me too, but skip the tomatoes," Mark said.

"Big man?" Tim said looking at Mag.

"You know what, double that order," Mag quickly replied.

"Wow, that was easy. Any more to drink and…" Tim paused and looked away, then quickly back to them. "Gotta asked you guys, what the hell are you all talking about? You look like you're deciding the fate of this country."

All three smiled as they looked at each other and then Mark said, "Much more than that."

"What's more than that?" Tim replied, and he looked curious as to what they were doing. Then he added, "Planning a robbery? There's a PNC down the street."

They each smiled, but only V replied, "No, we're not taking, my friend, we're giving. You'll have to pardon me for being the way I am because I'm overwhelmed. Over the past hours, I have had the most exciting, mind-boggling time of my life. I cannot describe it clearly. So, your establishment has provided a real contribution to our… discussion, which is the only way to describe what we have been doing. Maybe someday they'll be a plaque on your wall out there by the front door."

Tim smiled and said, "And what will it say, if I may ask?"

V quickly said with a broad smile, "In this establishment three people discovered the essence of humanity."

Tim seemed a bit stunned as he stepped back a couple of steps and then said, "What in the hell is… whatever you said, if I may ask?"

Mag smiled his huge smile and quickly replied,

"Where we've been and where we're going, my man."

Tim replied, "Well, I know one thing and that is that you all have been figuring all that out right here in my joint. Oh, keep it up, but I'm getting waved by the crew at the bar. Be back when we get your stuff done. Pretty busy right now, so it might be a while. Just hang in there. If you need something else in the meantime, just give me a wave," he said as he turned to go back to the bar.

Mark replied, "Will do and thanks for all you've done for us," he said to Tim who headed away from them. Then he said to Mag and V, "You know, been thinking about what you said just now Mag about where we've been and where we're going," as he paused, then said, "Yesterday I explained my medical situation, but I also have a couple other situations related to where I've been that I need to resolve because of my medical problem."

V's face tightened up as she said, "Is it bad?"

Mark smiled slightly and replied, "Ultimately… very bad and very complicated."

Mag's jaw tightened and his head dropped as he said quietly, "Ultimate bad, eh?"

Mark responded, "That's where I was this morning. Got, maybe, six months to live, but as I told you, they are offering me a new, difficult procedure that might add years if…that's the key word… if they can stop the cancer from spreading elsewhere. It's a unique procedure."

Mag looked away from him and straight at V. "Well, how we all going to handle that?"

V paused, looking at Mag, then turned to Mark and said, "Maybe just the way we look at our universe and our lives. Question though? No offense, Mark, but do we, or you, want more out of our existence, or is enough, enough. Isn't suffering just another part of our continual aging life existence until we leave our human element?"

Mag smiled and said, "That's one way, our way, of thinking of existence, ours ending."

Mark joined in, "Well it's a bit easy for you to say, but you're right. What we have discussed today has honestly calmed me down. Worse comes to worse, there will be no judgement needed. I will just return to where I and everyone else came from... up there somewhere or nowhere," as he looked up and out the window at the back of the bar. Then he looked back at V and added, "Here we are in this earthly bar that we humans escape to, avoiding the reality of our limited existence by sipping some booze to repress our thoughts of reality for a while."

"Wow, you are on a roll," V quickly interjected.

Mark quickly responded, "Well, maybe not a roll, but as we are being honest, I must let you know that life, the one we know, and in my case my life, may soon end as it is supposed to."

V's face tightened and she, for the first time, reached across the table and put her hand over Mark's hand. It was quiet between them, and then she said, "Well, that time is going to come for all of us, so let's work on that part of our existence." She put her other hand on Mark's hand and added, "What better time or company would you want to be with as you react to this situation, than now, with us."

Mag said quickly, "Right on, V." He then put his hands over both of their hands and said, "You got us, my man, so let's see what we can do about it."

Mark paused as V and Mag looked directly at him before responding, "I'm blessed having you two." After a second of silence he said, "Okay, as I said before, it's my pancreas. Cancer, bad. My doctors, my PC, who is also a cancer researcher and Dr. Wisnewski, who is a specialist in pancreatic cancer surgery, have given me a few months if not treated and maybe, the big maybe, if I try this new surgical reduction method they call it, might, key word might, stop the spread. As I said, I have decided to go with the surgery, so maybe I'll have a year or more, if this new surgical method has any affect." He paused, looked away and then back to his two new compatriots in life and said, "Ironic, eh. Here we are creating a new philosophy on life and I'm telling you now, I have maybe six months left in this body without surgery, but more if I have this procedure. Ironically, just what we have talked about has made me absolutely positive about the surgery. "'Screw it, do it,' as an old cab driver friend of mine always said when a decision had to be is made."

Neither V nor Mag responded for seconds until V, who had kept her hands over Mark's said, "He's right, Mark, and we're with you. You're going ahead with the new method, old man, so we'll go with you as much as we can," as she tightened her grip on his hands.

For the first time in minutes, they all smiled, and Mark put his free hand on top of V's hands, quickly joined by Mag's massive fingers. It was a pyramid of hands.

They were silent for seconds until Mark said slowly, "There is something else I have to lay on you two which is strictly opposed to our newfound philosophy…it's about a human trait of abundance which I have suffered from for years."

V looked at him with a questionable twist of her lips and said, "Abundance of what?"

"The curse of money…of wealth…of fear, maybe of…I don't know what…the more I think about it, I have all three," Mark quietly said.

V and Mag looked away from Mark, then at each other. V finally said, "Well, let's take care of this curse you talk about and make it into what the church I used to go to called 'a blessing,' Okay?"

CHAPTER TWENTY-TWO

As the three sat quietly after Mark's disclosure of his medical situation and began to talk about what he called a curse, Tim walked up and said, "Sorry to interrupt, but guys, hang in there your stuff is just about done. If you want more of anything, let me know now so I can add it to your order." He looked at them when they didn't respond and said, "You guys all right? For three people who never stop talking, you're awful quiet."

Mark responded, "No, we're just contemplating… life."

"Well, as long as your contemplating, I guess you're all right. Be back in a few minutes. If you want anything else, put up your hands like you're back in school, if you can remember that?" Tim said, chuckling and turning back toward the bar.

The three were silent for a few seconds and then V said, "Okay, Mark, you were talking about a curse, and you said money, wealth and you added fear. Could you elaborate what you meant?", she said.

Mark looked away and back at them when Mag, whose face was solemn as he looked away and then turned and met Mark's eyes as he said, "Mark, my man, whatever you gotta do we're with you. You hear me brother?"

"Loud and clear, but what I have to lay out for you two next, is something you may not believe," Mark quietly said.

V smiled and said, "Nothing would surprise me after what we have been talking about, so lay it on us."

"Yeah, man, let's hear it," responded Mag.

Mark sat back and straightened his back as he looked at both V and Mag as he said, "I've mentioned this to Mag, but I've got close to 20 million dollars in my bank in Switzerland. What am I supposed to do with it now that I may not be around to spend it or use it or do something with it?" His new life partners didn't blink or act surprised. They just looked at him. Finally, Mark went on, "Yeah, over the years, most of what I ever made just went into my bank. Made a lot and never really spent much, so it's just in my bank account in Geneva."

V replied slowly, "So, based on what you talk to us about for hours on end, you literally worked alone to achieve that financial…" she paused and said, "stability, right?"

Mark quickly replied, "Yes, just me for all these years, about fifty, at that. Oh, and another thing. While we have been talking all these hours about humanity, like I have never done in my life before, I noticed a few minutes ago, seven calls on my silent twelve-hundred-dollar cell phone. Six of them by a woman, Marsha

McDonough, who has been involved over the years in my financial success. She has been incredible during my situation here and actually has handled a couple of my outstanding big ones very well that I couldn't. Marsha is a real friend, so I will give her an update. The other person is a guy a bit younger than me, Trevor, who I've known most of my life and a pain in the ass. But I'll get back to him, some time." He paused and added," but after all we have discussed and decided upon about this life of ours, I have no desire to call him back, but I will get back to Marsha. She is probably my only real friend, other than you two out of the blue folks. But, back to my dilemma with all this money stored away, frankly, you guys can have it or find a good way to use it."

V looked to Mag at her side and then said quietly, "Mark, we just met physically, but I sense that I have known you for a lifetime. What you…", she paused then continued, as she glanced over at Mag and said, "you, Mag, and I, have talked for hours which seem to me like a lifetime because I have been affected like I have never been before. Oh, I have taught for years. College, high school, private, volunteered for folks for…forty years or so, and in the hours, I have listened to you and my young friend next to me, I have never felt more relaxed about the meaning of life. I've listened to two stories; one of an older man with individual effort and without any parental life guidance apparently, who achieved monetary wealth," as she paused, took a deep breath and went on, "and the other, a young black man, with tremendous parental guidance from two women, his mother and her mother, who has lived, suffered and miraculously revived himself with no material or monetary wealth.

I mean, what could represent the epitome of quality human lives more than you two men with completely opposite life stories." She paused and said, "I don't believe in blessings or any religious stuff, but meeting Mag and you has made me realize that the Universe, as absolutely physical as it is, somehow, somewhere, in some ethereal method, is aware of humanity here and elsewhere within its vast community. What the hell it is, I can't fathom, but this energy brought Mag to me and he to you, Mark." She paused and added, as her two cohorts had frozen expressions, "we must recognize each other's life situations and come up with a plan for our existence. For me, I don't know, maybe twenty years. For Mag, maybe fifty years, and for you, old man," she said with a loving smile, looking deep into Mark's face, "Oh, maybe five, ten, or fifteen more earth years. Truth being, we don't know any number of years for any of us."

Her last line caused her two cohorts to break into smiles that hadn't been seen for a while and Mark to respond, "I'll take them, young lady, for sure."

Mag added, "Whew, can't wait to create these years ahead," he said.

Mark added, "Well, if I have even five, or ten, fifteen more years, I guess I'd better call my doc's right now get that procedure asap," he paused then said, "as the same one of my old customers used to say about making a difficult decision, 'what the hell,' if you'll pardon the adjective or whatever it is."

"That's a perfect adjective," V responded. "Absolutely."

CHAPTER TWENTY-THREE

Tim brought their order over and they sat back, relaxing for the first time in quite a while. Mark said to them that he would call his doctor and go ahead with the operation and V and Mag nodded their agreement.

Mag was wolfing down his first cheeseburger and, wiping the mayo off his cheek and as he chewed, he looked at Mark and noticed he had a concerned look. "You okay, boss man?"

Mark looked at Mag and said, "Oh, yes, I was just thinking about all that I've gone through it such a short time, but I'm glad I am going to give it a go with the operation."

V pushed her sandwich away from her, straightened up her wide, shapely body and said slowly, "Well, that's courageous Mark and you know we're with you." She paused, smiled, and said, "You know I cannot believe I am sitting here, completely immersed in the lives of two men, one of whom I've never even met before today. It's incredible."

Neither Mark nor Mag responded as Tim yelled over to them, "You guys okay over there?"

All three waved their arms in an okay sign and Mag took another bite; V took a drink from her glass; and Mark played with his plate, not yet biting into his sandwich. V said, "Better eat something, you know. Gonna need some nourishment in a few days."

At that moment as they sat silent, a buzz was heard in Mark's pocket. He pulled out his cell phone and looked at it for a few seconds and leaned over to read a message. He looked at his phone for a short time and then he tapped it and put it in his pants pocket. He looked at his two compatriots and said, "You won't believe who that was." Not waiting for a response, he went on, "It was my banker in Switzerland giving me my current balance. Sorry guys, I was wrong, I don't have, what did I say, around twenty million …well anyway, its twenty-five and a half million."

It was quiet for a few seconds and then V responded, "Well, Mark, you got to have someone you want to give it to or something you want to use all that money for. I mean, after you get your operation, who knows, you may go back to work," V replied in a serious mode.

Mag added, "Man, from what you laid out for us these past hours and me yesterday, you are the man. You have done…" he paused, "so much in your work years, you'll get through this pancreas stuff and be back settling deals."

Mark straightened up and smiled, "Wow, what a team we turned out to be. I sort of want to cry, a bit. I have never…never had anyone believe in me for who I am, not what I do for them."

V quickly replied, "Well, I think we should finish this luxurious meal and continue our chatting," she paused and then said, "what a combo. A dying older man, a, what should I say, middle-aged old bag, and a young black dude recovering from himself. What a trio, yet I think we are on to something. So, let's finish our grub and get on with it."

Mag jumped in, as he said, "Burgers first, and life second. That's the way it should be, from my perspective. We'll get to you old man because I got some ideas you all won't believe. But pardon me a sec," as took a bite of his second jumbo-sized burger.

Ironically Mark and V both stood up and laughed as they interrupted each other saying they were heading for the rest rooms. Mag was finishing his second burger and laughed as he watched them heading for the rest rooms. He sat alone, finishing his burger and both were back in a few minutes.

As they sat back Mark, laughed, and said, "Wow, we got to the bathroom at the same time, V. We are a team for sure," which caused a breakout of laughter from them all. He then said, "I've been thinking about all that money in Switzerland and what I should do with it, but I'd rather get back to our philosophy we've been talking about," as he paused and said, "I mean we're living in this man-made Twenty-First Century and what is it, in relation to its home here on Earth, in this the Universe?"

Mag said, "Wow, that's sort of what I've been thinking about and what you two have been going on about. Man is just a physical being, a separate creation of natural elements and when our physicality ends, we, or people, call it death. Is that close?"

V immediately said, "Yeah, you said it. We're just temporary physical creations, that's all. No more, no less."

Mark replied quickly, "Sorry to change where you're going but it made me think of my temporary physical situation. What I'd like to do, now that I've decided to go for the procedure…" Mark paused, looked away at the bar and then back to the two of them, "Is for us to concentrate on our belief system that we've been talking about, which, by the way, ironically, ties in to my going for the operation. A temporary physical reaction within my own temporary physical existence. Which gets me to a question about our belief system that we've been working on. How do we think humanity fits into this Universe? How about you starting us off, V?"

V paused for a few seconds and then said, "Well, it has been quite a session over these past hours. It seems like weeks since we first started our exploration. You know, it got me thinking about what I saw just the day before yesterday. Have any of you seen the pictures coming from the James Webb Space Telescope?"

Mark replied, "No, I haven't. I remember it blasting off but haven't been watching any TV lately."

Mag added, "Me neither. All I've seen on TV are the game shows at a place I got some food the past weeks, oh and a couple ball games on the screen here. What's it all about?"

V answered, "Well, listening to you two and myself, my brain, the timing of what it is sending back to us, is almost like what we were talking about and agreeing with. The incredible magnified view of this Universe and what it is discovering. My God, the billions, and billions of potential planetary spheres that sure as hell look like what we are living on. I mean, who knows? Looks to me, this mere human, that this Universe is endless."

Mag responds, "Read somewhere at the Y, some science book, that in reality, we, us humans, have no idea what outer space is all about. It may be endless. We may be just one tiny sphere in an endless..." he pauses, "can't think of the right word for no beginning, no end. Each day we wake up and live a new day, then sleep, then wake up and on and on we go, as humans on this Earth in this endless as you said, V, Universe."

It was quiet for a few seconds and Mark said, "You know, from what we've been talking about, we're just alive, as we call it, for moments in the Universe. Not just us humans, but everything created is...momentary is all I can think of. Each day we spend alive is in itself a life, a beginning, a middle and an end. As I said before, each day is a life, in a way."

CHAPTER TWENTY-FOUR

The three sat quietly and finally V spoke up. "You know, we're getting close. I really think we nailed it, but there's something we must overcome."

"What's that?" Mag injected.

V quickly said, "We are human; we are what we call alive; we can talk like we have been living this life, but still, we must, no, we have to grab a hold of this consciousness in this life of ours." She paused, "I know what I just blurted out sounds complicated, but we, as humans, only talk about our existence as life. To me, this living experience we have had and will have, we, us three, must create and decide to use this time of life remaining, if, in fact, it is only remaining without any life after our physical death…we must create and work to achieve the most fulfillment out of this existence we have on this Earth, in this Universe."

"Whew," Mark said, "you nailed it. We can't sit here and postulate about life, the Universe, humanity, and our beliefs without accepting the absolute uniqueness of this existence we have on this tiny planet. An existence that has yielded the brainpower to come up with these beliefs of the life, humanity, and the Universe we are living in for such a short period of time." He paused and wiped his forehead with a handkerchief pulled from a pocket before adding, "So, we must accept our place in this Universe that we believe is endless; on this Earth; and most critically this time space for what it is and come up with a plan for ourselves and maybe others, to find individual peace and fulfillment."

"Whew," exclaimed Mag. "You summed it up well, old man."

Mag's playful and enthusiastic agreement made them all smile for the first time in a while. It was quiet until Mark said, "Old man, right, Mag, but you know, this whole concept we've been working on has fired me up and as I said earlier, I'm going to call that doc now and set up the goddamn operation, whadda ya think, partners?"

V replied with a huge smile on her usually serious face, "Do it and we'll be with you all the way. Once that's done, we're going to make some plans for each of us and for us together because I know you will beat that… that crap that's inside you."

"Couldn't have said it better myself," Mag added. He turned and looked at the clock over the bar and said, "Hey, man, call them now, eh?"

Mark pulled out his cell phone, fiddled with it for a few seconds and then tapped in a number. In a few seconds he was connected and talked quietly for a few minutes. V and Mag sat silently as he talked. Then Mag leaned over and said something to V. She straightened up, looked over at Mark, then back to Mag, then said something quietly to him. They both leaned back in their chairs as Mark finished his call and put his phone back in his pocket.

"Well?" V asked.

Mark replied, "They want me to come in tomorrow morning to do some testing and a special type of MRI, specifically for the procedure that they will be doing. Some new one designed at the hospital for this type of operation. I told them I will do it."

V responded, "Well, gents, we got a bit of time left in the day, so we got one thing to settle. Our main man is going for it, so we can think about what we, our newfound group, are going to do with the rest of our lives, whatever time frame that is."

Mag said, "You know, what you just said is right on. Time frame; life; it's limited. Could be an hour; a day; a month; maybe some years, no matter how old we are at this very moment. So, what we have been discussing fits right in. We ain't got a clue how long our minds and bodies will be on this earth.", as he paused and said, "Sorry, I could go on and on about what we got and what we haven't got, but I do know we got…n-o-w. Now is all we got."

Mark smiled widely, not his usual facial expression, and responded, "I really like that, Mag. Now is it, so whatever happens to me with this procedure and eventually my physical life, every moment of that will be just a connection of now's." He paused again as V and Mag looked at him awaiting more, then he added, "Remember the saying, 'now or never,' wow that says it all except, we haven't figured out what never means, have we?"

V responded, "Never doesn't exist, Mark. It's just a human excuse. The only thing us beings can count on is what Mag just said: 'Now.'"

They were quiet. Then Mark spoke up. "Speaking of now, I think we're on the right track and whatever happens to me with this operation, I want for us to figure out a way to handle all this wealth, accumulated over the years. There has to be something we can do together to use it to those who have nothing on this Earth…those who need a foundation to have a chance. Know what I mean?"

Mag replied, "Brother, you nailed it. Our mantra…" he laughed, smiled, and turned away for a few seconds, but turned back and continued "A chance; a word a dude taught me at the Y, couple months ago. He was a druggie, gone straight. Bud, oh crap, can't think of his last name. Anyway, Bud had taught Buddhism and was. in the Himalaya's for a couple years where he learned what became his life religion until he started taking drugs that ended up just about killing him. Bud was a neat dude. He hadn't done drugs in three years when I met him, but craved them, for the brief escape from thinking about life, but he said, death was his greatest fear. Now, Bud, was then working part-time in a pizza joint in downtown during the pandemic when nobody wanted to work. He said to me the virus was the best thing that had happened to him since he stopped taking drugs, which as I said was almost a three-year time frame. He was literally down and out, but had "found his life," as he put it so well. But Bud, regained his Buddhist training and even though he was making little money, his mind was solid, and he was, what he called 'happy.' He laughed when he said 'happy,' because now he knew what that word meant; it meant to him, contentment; because he knew how he wanted to live the rest of his life. Thinking back to Bud, you two, Mark and V, that's us now. Mark we can use those funds to help folks find a path in life for those who need a chance."

Mark smiled and replied, "It will work, you two, it will work. We will give those folks a chance on this Earth."

CHAPTER TWENTY-FIVE

It had been five weeks since the Trio, as they ended up calling themselves, had sat at their table in The Bystander. Two days after their last session, Mark had the procedure to remove the cancerous area in his prostrate utilizing the new digitally controlled surgical device that carefully isolated and cut away the affected area. The doctors thought, based on their post operative analysis of the cancer, that it was a less invasive cancer which meant he might be protected from recurrence.

Mag and V had visited him almost every day he was in the University Hospital until he was discharged. Mark had only his apartment-office on Mt. Washington in Pittsburgh to stay in when he got out, but it did have a small bedroom that he stayed in as he recuperated from the operation. It worked fine for him where he could rest and still have a kitchen with the basics that looked down on his city. V had cooked meals for him as he got into a routine of resting, working a bit on the phone and online with Marsha, who needed his help with some outstanding contracts that had come in and she has asked Mark to set up his brand of settlement that she could work on.

Mag had moved into a small apartment in the same building where V lived in the North Side. During the weeks of Mark's recovery period, he and V had begun a workshop with volunteers from both the YMCA and the YWCA to create job systems for down and out folks to start slowly figuring out an area where they might find a work situation. In these days of young folks seemingly wanting to go against the age-old process of picking professions or type of work for life, the new age of just doing odd jobs to pay for rent and food seemed to be enough for many of the young generation.

Mag and V were trying to develop a way to help folks, especially young ones, to become independent, yet be able to provide safely for themselves. As he recovered, Mark jumped in by setting a fund to cover costs. So, by the time he was able to get around and out of his apartment, the three had begun a business venture that was to become a new, positive venture for them and many folks seeking stability and possible meaningful lives. Mark recovered a bit quicker than his doctors thought, as he felt so much better, mostly his psychological self than his physical self, which he knew would be in his continual thought mechanism.

He remembered clearly what Doctor Wisniewski had said to him as he was finally leaving the hospital room where he had been. "Time will tell," was his old-fashioned response. In seven days, he had been discharged and this afternoon, a month later, he was back in their bar booth, awaiting the rest of the Trio, both of whom had visited him in the hospital usually every day during his recouperation after the surgery.

The bar had a few young people, quietly sipping their drinks and enjoying their sandwiches. It was quiet and he felt alone, a feeling he hadn't experienced much over the years because his brain usually focused on more productive and practical thoughts.

Mark sat there and suddenly a new thought took over which caused him to reach into his back pocket and pull out his leather-bound notebook. When he was lying in his hospital bed, for some reason, he thought about the haiku poetry he used to write whenever something hit him that he thought could be his version of the three-line Japanese style poetry that he really liked.

'Haven't done a haiku in years and so much has gone on,' he thought to himself. So, he got comfortable in the booth seat and pulled out his pencil, screwed up the lead and twiddled with it as he looked at the blank page of his well-worn notebook. Mark could see the last poems in the notebook he had written when he was in Thailand on a work venture, three years ago. The last one he read twice because it predicted somewhat what he'd gone through with his operation and hospital stay. The last line made him smile:

'Worry, brings tension', were the words he'd written that night in his hotel room. He remembered why he'd written the three-line poem and why the last sentence had meaning to what he was going through now. The haiku was written because he was worried by the solution to the problem between two companies, one an Indian company and the other Chinese. He suggested a solution to the Indian rep, which he accepted and then he suggested to Yee Chang, representative of the Chinese company, to tell his superiors that they should accept the offer accepted by the the Indian company. He remembered waiting for Yee Chang's decision and was worried how the company would react. Chang, he knew, was closely associated to the Chinese government, as was the company, so would they give up anything worried him. He wrote the poem in his hotel room awaiting their decision. As his finished the last line of his haiku, his cell phone had buzzed, and Chang called him to tell him the company had accepted the deal. He remembered how he laughed at his last line of the haiku that he had just written that night and hadn't looked at in over a year.

Now Mark was back in the corner of the bar where his whole life had been revitalized, not only from the operation but from actual friendships with two fascinating people with whom he had created a powerful belief system. He looked down at the leather notebook and pulled out the small lead pencil and began to write a haiku about how he felt. Slowly, words came to him, and he wrote out a sentence in a few seconds, followed by a longer second line which was then followed by a shorter, ending sentence. He sat back, picked up the notebook with both hands and just stared at what he wrote. Then, out loud, quietly, he read what he had written hurriedly:

OUT OF NOWHERE

Life is moving right along,
Then, wham you're slammed to hell;
Maybe heaven?"

Mark pushed the notebook away from him and looked over at the bar where laughter within the young folks sitting there broke out uproariously. He looked back at his notebook and re-read the quick poem he'd just written. He felt dissatisfied, and he took his pen and crisscrossed over what he'd written. Then he sat back, thoughtful.

"Jesus, have I lost my touch," he said. Fiddling with the pencil, he turned the page and flattened it out. Sitting back, he was still, just looking down at the notebook. Then he took the pencil and started to write:

NOW WHAT?

For my seven decades
I've lived my life as I wanted:
Now, no more?

Again, he sat back and looked down at the freshly written words. Slowly with the pencil he crossed out the third line and restarted:

NOW WHAT?

For my seven decades
I've lived my life as I wanted:

He kept looking at the empty third line, and couldn't find a finish, so he put down his pencil, sat back, and just kept looking at the blank third line. As he sat silently, a shadow came over him. He looked up at Mag standing there with a smile. Neither spoke and then Mag said, "What's up, my man. You look like your far, far away."

Slowly Mark's head rose, and he replied, "You're a

mind reader because I am far away, yet I'm looking for a couple words for right here," as he tapped his notebook.

Mag said, "Right where?"

"Here," Mark repeated, as he tapped his notebook again and then handed it to Mag. "See those first two sentences?"

Mag looked down at the notebook that Mark put in front of him and said, "Yeah, I see a couple lines. So?"

Mark said, "Give me a couple words for the third line based on the first two."

Mag leaned closer and his lips moved as he read the first two lines slowly. He then looked up at Mark and said, "How about…" he paused, then said, "Keep living."

Mark put the pencil in his mouth and moved it up and down as he looked at the blank poem. Slowly he took the pencil and wrote in 'Keep living' and put down the pencil.

Neither spoke for a few seconds then Mag said, "Man you…we ain't got no choice. You gotta keep living as best you can, know what I mean?"

Mark for the first time in a while slowly smiled and replied, "I know what you mean, Mag, I sure do."

Incredibly, as they were mired in reflection about what had just transpired, up walked V, with a large leather notepad. She stood beside Mag, leaned over, and tapped his arms and said, "Nice to see you, M man".

Mag looked at her and said, "Well, our good friend here is trying to finish a tiny poem he wrote, and he needs some words. I gave him two," keep living."

Mark turned the notebook, so it was in front of V and said, "Here, give it a shot."

V picked up the notebook and slowly read the poem once and then again. Then she wrote next to Mag's two words, "Keep living."

She put down the notebook and looked over at Mark and said, "How about, now our way."

LIFE

In my seven decades
I've lived my life. my way.
Keep living Now, our way!

Mark said quietly, "Better, I'm leaving both as a memento. Thanks to both of you. As I think about what you both suggested, it made me realize that whatever life I have left, I must live it, as Mag said to me last week, "full throttle". I have to work with life instead of believing I am in total control. I am not and I realize that now, maybe for the first time in my life." He smiled and added, "Thanks, you two; you've got me out of a doldrum that I'd created and frankly have never suffered from before." Then he sat back, smiled, and added, "It's so great to be back at our table and you know the more I think of the lines I wrote, the more I don't like them. Gotta work on what I am trying to say, or write."

V responded quietly, as she backed away from Mag," And what are you trying to say, or write, Mark?"

"Ah, great question. The bottom line, eh?" Mark replied.

"Yep, isn't that essential?" V replied.

"It is, it is," Mark replied, then paused before saying, "You know, I was upset because I hadn't written anything in years and this time is the most critical, I think I have ever faced. Much more than any big deal I was going to lose or a possible plane accident I faced a couple times as I flew around the world. No, this moment of my life is the absolute most crucial time in my life simply because I may soon die," as he paused and added almost angrily, "You see what I just said is wrong, so wrong. I may not die soon. I may have a lot more time going for me."

Mag said softly, "Well my man, what you just said is the man I know. You are going to live on because me and the V lady are going to help you do it." He looked over at V and went on, "We're with you, which is so strange, don't yuh think. I mean just weeks ago, if you had been in this situation, you would have been all by yourself. Now you got us to help you, so, wow, something is working in this Universe of ours to bring us to you at this time, don't you think?"

Mark smiled broadly and replied, "You don't know how great that is for me to know that I have you two." He paused and looked at his old notebook and said, "I'll leave your lines here and start to add some more haiku in the coming days to this old notebook of mine. I'm sure many lines will hit me with you two in my life", as he put the notebook back into his back pocket.

The three became quiet as the noise picked up in the bar. Then V spoke up as she looked at the bar and then back to Mark and Mag, saying, "Well, normalcy is returning to our venue, and I think to us too. Here we are trying to write a bit of poetry when I'm here to find out how the hell you are doing today. I mean, my newest best friend had a new and experimental procedure to extend your life and we're working on poetry. You must be on the road to recovery."

Mark responded, "I am, V, I am. As they told you in my room, it went perfectly but they won't know for weeks or maybe months if they have stopped any new cancerous invasion. But strangely, I feel really damn good. Physically and mentally, for sure. And I, we, have some work to do. I got all these calls coming in from Marsha about big deals people she wants me to see if I can solve, but somehow, I have to let her know I won't be able to help her much anymore because I have a different life role to play now, thanks to you two. So, what do you say, we think of something for us to do to spread the word of our Universal vision and talk more about utilizing all those funds I have? My poetic lines will come from my new view of life and you two."

"Well, speaking of those lines, what were you trying to write with that poem?" asked V.

Mark smiled and said, "Excellent question. You know, V, you and Mag have come from out of the blue and empowered me to accept my situation and move forward. What I'd written I now realize was negative in a way, and what I'm going to write now and, in the days, ahead will be absolutely positive," he said, taking the notebook back out of his rear pocket and placing it right in front of himself on the table. He then turned the page from what he had written and began to write on the next page. V and Mag look at each other. Mag shrugged his shoulders and smiled slightly at V, who sat back watching Mark writing in the notebook.

Mark sat writing in the notebook for a few minutes as V and Mag just watched. Finally, he put down the pencil and pulled up the notebook, then said. "Let me read this to you two, okay?"

CHAPTER TWENTY-SIX

After he had read the new poem, he put down the notebook and looked across to his two new friends.

No one spoke for a few seconds, then V quietly said, "You know it's amazing how you can explain a life situation in so few words," she paused and added, "I'd love you to read what you just wrote, Mark?"

Mag spoke up before Mark could respond, saying, "You know, it's so funny how a sudden and life-threatening event can stop you cold, making you realize how temporary life on this Earth is. Yet, look at you. Know what I mean?"

"I do, Mag, I do. Very eloquent, Mag and right on," Mark responded as he picked up the notebook. Then he said, "Okay, let me read this one, and slower." He read…

LIFETIME

Lifetime is a short time,
You come, you live, you go;
A Universal moment!"

V smiled and said, "You said, or I should say, you wrote it all, Mark? That's all there is, yet it is so much and yet so little, but no matter…it is everything."

Mark, expression solemn, said, "Thanks, I think it captures in those few words what we have been talking about. Not negative at all, but so positive, I think."

"Right on, my man, you captured it so very well," Mag said, reaching across the table and tapping his wrist.

Mark straightened up and said, "Okay, enough of me, I'm feeling really good, especially being back at our table, together. So, it's been all about me and now you two, let's talk about what's next for us. I mean we have sort of become a tiny force of nature, so to speak, but with that, we must accept and realize each of us, individually, must live a life. Pardon my preaching, but you know, no one knows what percolates in the mind of anyone else. V and I do not know your macro mind Mag and you don't know either of ours. I have a great positive sense of both of you, but deep within the recesses of your brains is your reality of existence. I will never know your internal thoughts, nor you mine, but we do have an external exposure of ideas and actual living activities. Things you do; things you say, and things you perform; all your external self; and we seem to have accepted each other's external selves, so to speak. Make any sense to you guys?"

V immediately said, "Yes, I've been thinking a lot over the past days about meeting back up with you two again. It's solidified my belief system. Have no plans to go to a monastery and preach or anything, but I think it's a powerful, true assessment of what humanity is and isn't."

"You took some thinking away from me, V," Mag said. "Been working on a life plan for me that ties in with what we've been formulating. Know what I mean?" he asked.

Mark and V agreed in unison. Then V said, "You know what you said Mark, ties in exactly with what I've been thinking about the last few days. Must say, first, I was hoping that you'd continue to get through your procedure okay, Mark, but also something hit me that ties in with what Mag just said. That is that we humans are and have been and will be created in the future only by the Universe. No more, no less."

Mark responded. "You know, even though I've been tied up a bit figuring out what to do with myself after the procedure, I was listening to a couple of the nurses in the hospital that were helping me as they talked about their church, and I realized that religion is still a powerful human force. We all know it from our childhood. Watching European and Asian shows streaming online, as I do, I'm aware that billions of humans for centuries believe in a religion with a God that controls everything. So, during my recouping days these past weeks, I realized this age-old belief system ties in with what we were talking about in our sessions before my operation. That is, God may just be a name for the Universe. The Universe may be God. Make any sense, guys?"

V slapped the table and said, "You are right on, Mark right on. Had the same thought as I listened to some of my folks, I work with who are in all kinds of religions, or none at all. They all, though, talk a bit about some type of God figure, or something that is controlling their life and the world itself."

Mag leaned forward and said, "So ironic you two are saying this, because I was talking to this preacher who comes into the 'Y.' He was going on about Jesus and the God that he believed in and how it was so appropriate to the today's world. I asked this preacher, who is a pretty normal preacher dude, not like those TV dudes, if he thought Jesus and God believed in anything close to what I've and we've been talking about. I had already given him a bit about our belief in the ultimate and unknown power of the Universe. It was ironic, because he paused and said, "The Universe you brought up… is God.""

Mark smiled and said, "To be expected. In a way, though, God is a man-made word for a single entity controlling all of the Universe or whatever one calls the endless vacuum filled with billions and billions of unending existences of elements in various conditions. There is no human word to describe it or understand it. No one has a clue what the Universe is or if it was ever created from nothing or somehow has always been in existence. And I guess we are all simply physical sons and daughters created after millions of years of elements blending together into what we call humans. If you think, Mag, that this preacher could listen to us, go get him, bring him over."

All three laughed lightly. Then Mag said, "That was quite an explanation you laid on us, my man. I don't think he could handle it, but I might. If I can repeat to him what you just said, I'll see his reaction. Truthfully, I'd say he'd pass."

V responded quickly, "He probably would for

sure, but I think now we just got to take a deep breath or breaths and concentrate on what we have entered into…this new world, so to speak.”

"So, to speak, I like that," Mark said, "and I agree. I got some things I want to talk to you about. But first, I have to get this off my chest. Our Universe is the macro situation, but over the past days, I have been astounded by my situation, the micro situation." He straightened up and said, "Okay, here I am, an older white man who has obviously succeeded in this absolutely weird world created by a humanity which might last hundreds or thousands more years after formulating from thousands, probably millions of years. Why? Because we, humanity, I think is out of touch with the Universe. And me, I have been too, out of touch for my whole life on this planet. Now I realize it, at a time when my life is in danger of ending. But what these days have made me realize is that humanity is exploring the universe a bit, but meanwhile, also destroying the planet it's situated on. Then I've thought about myself, in this life of mine, as I followed a nasty trail of simply making human money which sits in a bank in Switzerland, useless. What the hell am I going to do as a human, a person in my coming days of fulfillment and reality and what do I do with all my begotten money stashed away in a bank."

It was quiet for a few seconds and then Mag said, "Well, partner, I think we gotta make what we have discovered together about life fit with your funds that are stashed away. Somehow, we three must come up with some way to use what you have stashed away to put our belief system to work in helping folks find their way in this world. We need a plan. As grandma used to tell me all the time, 'Son, you gotta have a plan and follow it.' So, you two, let's do it, let's come up with a plan, eh?"

CHAPTER TWENTY-SEVEN

They did decide to work on a plan. From that moment, as they sat around the table in the bar, which had become their headquarters, the three huddled around yellow legal pads and worked on a plan for each of them respectively and for all of them together. Their objective was to create and find fulfillment for themselves individually, for their group and their shared philosophy, and to help their fellow humans understand their beliefs. For these three folks from different backgrounds, upbringings, and life stories, so much of life crystallized in their talking over the past days with each other.

The experience was almost like something out of the Bible, as V had said. She had grown up in a family that strongly believed in the Bible but had since drifted away from those beliefs after leaving her family in her early twenties. She now believed in living a good life and helping others and had found Mark and Mag to be a great help in this regard. She didn't see their arrival as a godsend in the traditional religious sense, but more like a force from the vast universe that she had immersed herself in. She believed that the universe was immense and that this force created endless power that made humans unique. Talking with Mark and Mag had been the most exciting thing to happen in her life for a long time.

The coincidence that brought these three people together was so unique that they felt it had been set up by some Universal force. Mark, a man who had made a fortune in his career was now faced with the challenge of finding a way to put his wealth to good use as he faced possible death. Then after hours and hours of talking about themselves and about their mutual beliefs, they agreed that they needed to create a plan to reflect their beliefs and focus on helping mostly the less fortunate members of society to find life fulfillment. They talked about how their country was in turmoil and almost controlled by the media whether it be television or social media. They talked and agreed that the current political climate was also very divisive, not only nationally, but in many local areas. Their belief that Mark's method of bringing opposing sides and folks together, might be an opportunity for them to become a middle source to settle some of these differences. However, before they could do anything, they needed to figure out how to transfer millions of dollars from a bank in Zurich to an American bank. They decided to use Guardian National, the largest local bank in Pittsburgh, where they planned to establish their headquarters. Sitting together in their small triangular booth at the back of the bar, they began to work out the details.

They'd been working non-stop for a few hours

when Mark spoke up", "Now that we got the beginnings of our plan settled, why don't we just talk about our thoughts while we were separated?" as he smiled and added, "I know I had some beauties."

"Funny you should say that because my mind never stopped thinking about what we have been…discussing. The only words I can think of to describe what we've been doing is… verbal workshop." V responded.

"Verbal workshop. I love it," Mark said. "V for verbal, eh?"

Mag piped up, "That's good, all right, but what got me going was that there is so much out there. Everyone, every human being, has a belief of some sort. Some religious, some ethnic, some environmental, and some just personal. But from what we've been uncovering between us, is that all belief is sub…servient, I think is the right word, to be subservient to the Universe that created us all and will take us all. Know what I mean?"

"Mag, I think you're headed for Tibet," V replied.

"I'm ready, but first I'm gonna stay in the 'Burgh," Mag quickly answered.

With that response, Mark looked across at the bar and waved at Tim who was gabbing with two young ladies. Mark waved again and this time Tim waved back and gave him a sign he would be over shortly. Mark then said to V and Mag, "It's been a while since you two ate and now thankfully, I'm hungry for the first time in quite a while, So, let's say we have a little bit of food as we start, folks, and then make some planning moves," as he paused then said, "You know I've been alone most of my life, but there was time during my rehab weeks, when I really missed you guys, you know…but okay, back to my point. Well, we got the funds transfer plan settled so I'll call my banker in Switzerland and have him transfer my funds, which will make him sad, and the bank up the street here very happy. I'll set up a meeting for tomorrow at the bank and would like you two to join me."

"Why us?" V responded.

"Well, based on what we have been talking about, I think we need to come up with a plan for utilizing the funds proactively to match our philosophy," Mark said.

Tim walked up with a wide grin on his face. "Well, what can I get for you three?"

V spoke up quickly and said, "You got any kind of a salad?"

Tim smiled, "I make terrific shrimp salads, believe it or not. How does that sound"

V laughed and said, "Hard to believe, but lay one on me Tim."

Tim replied, "I'm a bit offended by your response, but just wait and see," as he paused and said, "You two?"

Mag replied quickly, "Just a burger, double cheese with whatever you have and a diet Coke."

"Any soup left?", Mark asked.

"Believe it or not I have some potato soup that I made for tomorrow, but it's done.

How's that sound?" Mark replied.

"Perfect. I got some pain but not as bad as it was and finally, I'm really hungry, which is a good sign. I'll take a bowl of that soup and how about some decaf coffee, if you have any." Mark answered.

Tim replied, "I do, and I'll bring it over. Okay anything else."

Mag raised his hand as if he was in school and Tim looked at him, smiled, and said, "Yes, young man?"

"Double that soup, my man, and two decaf coffees," Mag quickly said.

Tim looked at them and said, "If you need anything else let me know because the joint is filling up," as he turned and walked back to the bar.

"Well, yes and no. I'm fine sitting here with you two, but having a bit of trouble with here," he said as he patted his gut.

V said, "What can we do for you?" as she straightened up.

"Oh, you can't really do anything. Called my doc's and they want to see me in the morning to double check me, but it's painful, but not as it was," Mark paused and added, "That's why I want to get my war chest taken care of."

"Well, don't think we're thinking about that, my man. We need you well. So, what can we do to help you, now?" Mag said seriously.

Mark responded, "We need to get our plan outlined and I think we've had a great start. What we have talked about, to me, is classical. It will be a message to so many hurting folks in this country of ours that hopefully we can bring reality and peace to them. I think our belief in the total power of the Universe, over all that we do as humans, with Gods or no Gods, is reality." He paused and his face scrunched up obviously in pain, "Sorry, got another grabber," as he pushed his lower stomach.

V stood up and leaned over Mark, who was bent over and said gently to him, "What's going on Mark. What can I do? Do we need to call someone?"

He quietly replied, "They told me I left too soon, but I felt pretty good considering. But I get these jabbing pains in my gut. Not as bad, but damn it, gotta keep going. Can't let this thing hold me or us back."

Mag, who had also gotten up, stood behind V and said quietly, "You are the man, for us, so you gotta hang in there. What can we do?"

They stood quietly as Mark hunched over. Then Tim walked back over to them and said, "What's up, you guys. Can I help?"

"Our main man is in pain…" Mag replied.

"Should I call someone?" Tim asked.

Mark slowly looked up at Tim, whose face was tight with a look of fear, "Thanks, Tim, thanks. No, it's going away, slowly. Thanks," he repeated as he straightened up.

Mag looked down at Mark and put his hand on V's arm. She looked at him and Mag nodded for her to step aside with him.

Mark sat back slowly, yet his face was still drawn with pain.

Mag and V moved back along the wall as Mark remained seated. V quietly said to Mag, "We have to get him to either his doctor's office or over to the hospital."

Mag quietly replied, "You're right. Let's just tell him what we want to do because we want to make sure he's okay."

"You, tell him, Mag. You got a way with words with him," V answered as she went over and sat down across from Mark who was now leaning over a bit in his chair again.

Mag walked back to him and said, "My man,

me and the boss lady here want to get you somewhere we can be sure you're going to be taken care of. Okay?"

Mark straightened up, smiled slowly, and said, "You two might have thought I was out of it, which I was for a minute or so, but honestly, I'm feeling better, and my mind started percolating again, so here is what I would like. Okay?"

Mag looked at V, who smiled slightly, and they both looked at Mark expectantly.

Mark sat up slowly and said, "I really do feel better and believe it or not, my mind got me thinking about what we're going to do with all that we have talked about since we first met, what feels like a couple of years ago, though I know it was only a month or so. But what's happened between us has been the most wonderful days of my life, believe me. I know what we three believe in and I also know that I trust you with my life. Not physically, which I do also, but with pursuing our life commitment that we have talked about. Sorry for the big mouth, but for some reason, although I hurt a bit, my mind is really fired up and I want to lay this out to you, in case...something happens. You with me?"

CHAPTER TWENTY-EIGHT

The three had finished their mid-day lunch. Mark even took a bite of Mag's burger, but now they were sitting back and relaxing at the table. Mark was sipping on his coffee, and he was relaxed as his pain had subsided, obviously feeling better. V and Mag sat across from him, their usual arrangement. It was quiet in the bar as it was almost empty as it was passed past the lunch hour.

Mark took a deep breath. "Been thinking, so okay, here goes." He wiped his face with his right hand and rubbed it into his right thigh. "Sorry, a little perspiration. Well, ever since I went into the hospital for my procedure and in the days since, I've never stopped thinking about us three. But mostly my mind focused on you Mag, primarily. Not to diminish the absolute love, affection, and closeness I feel for V, but as I looked at the future of this country, this world, and our threesome, I came to the conclusion that Mag, you must lead us." He stopped talking and looked right at

Mag and then to V before saying, as he looked back at Mag, "You have the youth. You have the life. You have the ability to lead our cause. Our cause…" He paused again, took a deep breath that seemed to cause him a bit of pain, yet he continued, "Our finding each other is a one in a billion occurrence. Why we met in this bar? I know it was supposed to happen. Why did you come in here, Mag? Again, it was supposed to happen. And lastly, why did you find V and bring her here, same answer. Because this unknown, most powerful, interactive universal network that we've been talking about, wanted it all to happen. But this is not a religion or some kind of voodoo, spiritual belief, it is the reality of human life." He paused again, took another deep breath, and continued. "Mag, you have to take us to the next page as in a novel of humanity itself. Your age, your life experience, your mind, and don't take this wrong way, but your race. I am the white folk and V is a bit of both. The white folks have done some great things within humanity but also some awful ones. You, my man, as you would say to me so well, are our future. You, with help from V, can take our message to the folks. It's a good one. I believe our message will be a true one for us humans on this tiny sphere in the unlimited mass of the Universe." He paused, took another deep breath, and said softly, "That's it for me."

V smiled as she reached for Mag's shoulder with one hand and across to Mark's shoulder with the other, then said, "I'm with you Mag and you as well, old man."

Her line cracked them up and mellowed the mood. It got them holding hands and it also got Mark to sit up with a huge smile on his creased face. "Old man, for sure, but you know, I ain't done. Got something left in me and somehow, I'm gonna beat this bastard inside of me," he said. Then he looked at Mag who was quiet, just looking back and forth at Mark and V. "So, Mag, you're. the man."

Mag looked at them both separately for a few seconds and said quietly, unusual for him, "Well, I'm overwhelmed but inside, so excited. I will do all I can to see us find our path to where we want to go and be. Thank, you two. I must admit, I am very proud of were going to do."

They were quiet for a few seconds as V leaned back and put her elbows on the back of the chair. Her large body was taut, then slowly began to soften as she relaxed, then smiled as she said, "Well, guys we got a couple hurdles to jump, as I see it. First, get this old dude across from me fixed up; second, figure out how we can help folks who need a boost in their lives. Somehow to reach out to folks who need to have a chance and help them have a more positive sense of what life is all about and not about. But also we need to do as Mark said before his procedure which is to find a way to utilize his resources," she paused and added, "for your info, money and all that goes with it has never been a part of my life, but so many folks can't even find a place to sleep; drink safe water; feed their babies, while this country's goddamn billionaires have gone from 70 to 700, or something like that. Jesus Christ almighty, what kind of a world do we live in."

Mark coughed, putting his right hand over his mouth, and then saying, "Lady, you nailed it. Life is so...so precious, is all I can say. So many who are conceived, born and live, are throwaways. They die before they can enjoy a sunset or smell a rose or touch the hands of one who loves them or whatever makes life so unique. Religions have created this myth or belief, whatever you want to call it, about heaven, so people, who live and fear death, think they're going to be transferred into some magic kingdom of existence. It's the Universe, folks. We are only beings created by minerals over billions of years and we are destined to simply return to a mineral existence in the ground, in the water, or poof, in the air." He paused and looked exhausted. Then he laughed as he added slowly, "And you know, you two, I ain't ready to go poof."

Mag and V looked at each other and laughed as they looked back at Mark, who beamed his first real smile in quite a while.

They were still laughing when Tim came up to them and said, "Okay, looks like you're okay now, boss man, so does the Mafioso need anything?"

The three laughed at Tim's line, then Mark said, "For me, when you have time, I'll take some more of that decaf coffee." Mag and V both said they didn't need anything, and Tim started to walk away, but turned, looked back, and said, "Here's something funny for you guys. A bit strange, I thought. A couple girls and guys who are sitting at the bar closest to you have been giggling to themselves the last few minutes. One of them leaned over and I heard her say to her friend, 'Those old dudes over there are planning something. We should slide our chairs over a bit and find out what they're planning." Tim smiled and added, "What's funny is that they did slide their chairs a bit closer and for minutes they were quiet. Then, suddenly, as I was walking by them, they broke out in laughter. What would you three say that would make them young ones laugh so hard?"

Mark smiled and replied gently, "Probably heard us laughing, which for us is a bit unusual." He paused, looked up at Tim and said, "Buy them a round on us and ask them if they could stop by for a chat with us, if they want to. We got something for them."

Tim smiled, turned, and walked back to the group of young ones who were watching from their stools. He talked to them and then they huddled, and one tall young boy could be heard saying, "What the..." as he got off the stool and came towards the trio at the table, followed closely by two young girls and another guy. The four walked up to the table. The first young man said, "What's up with you guys, anyway?"

From behind the bar, Tim stood back and looked at the group at the table and the four young ones standing almost at attention in front of them. He smiled slowly, looked back at the bar, which had just two people talking with beers in hand, and then looked back at this incredible picture at the booth. It looked like a painting by his favorite painter, Edward Hopper picture, as no one moved, and they were all silent.

Finally, Mark looked at Mag and nodded. Mag looked at V and she nodded. He straightened up his big body and said, "Welcome to our world, youngins. Saw you laughing at us at the bar and well, you were right on. Laughter is a release, you know. Gets any tension out of your mind. Not that any of you... Oh, by the way, how old are you guys and how about your first names..." he paused and said, "Oh, yeh, ours first. I'm

Mag, the youngest of this trio, mid-thirties and as you can see, one proud black dude." He points to Val and says," And that doll is Val, in her, oh well, over thirty, and the dude across from me is my main man, Mark. He's the old dude of this trio, but one wise old dude, I must say. Okay, so how about you guys?"

They looked at each other and then the blonde haired, tall boy said, "Ok, me, I'm Donald and just had my twenty-second birthday." He turned to the dark-haired, tall girl beside him. "Louise, your turn."

Louise's face tensed, then she smiled, "I'm Louise; nursing now, but headed for grad school," she said, turning to the girl next to her who straightened up.

"Michelle, and I'm also in nursing, but I'm shooting to be a doctor someday," the third one said. She then turned to the short, dark-haired boy next to her.

The shorter dark-haired boy slowly smiled and said, "My turn. Okay, I'm Reggie and I'm in law school. Went to high school with Donnie."

It's quiet again then Mag says, "Donnie, Reggie, Louise, and Michelle. Wow, what a neat group. You just having a lunch here today or is this a special day?"

Donnie spoke up, "Just celebrating my twenty-second birthday, a couple days late, that's all."

"So, you're twenty-two. Wow…" Mag paused, pulled his chin with his right hand, and seemed to be thinking for a few seconds and said, "My twenty-second I was in Afghanistan and was lying behind a wall while some dude was firing at me. But now I'm here, looking at you four young folks and upbeat about this little group meeting. Pretty neat. Three old folks and four young folks."

Louise interjected, "What are you three celebrating?"

Mag replied, "Our lives on …" he paused and then said, "What do you think?"

The four looked at each other and then Michelle piped up and said, "What do you mean?"

Mag quietly replied, "We were celebrating our lives on this earth and in our Universe. Which is most important to you all? Our earth or the Universe?"

Michelle looked at her three companions and then back at Mag with a puzzled look on her oval, soft face and then replied, "Earth, of course."

Mag responded, "You're right, physically, the Earth, but what about everything else out there?"

They did not respond as they looked at each other as if trying to figure out what was going on. Finally, Donnie piped up and said cockily, "What else, man, what else. It's all space, man. It goes on and on. That's it. Why should we care?"

"You don't have to," Mag quickly replied. "No, at your age, you got more important things to think about, like maybe getting a job, hooking up with someone, moving somewhere you've read about. All those things' folks your age are trying to figure out. Exciting things you see movies about," he paused and added, "What's funny is that some of the most popular movies for young people are space movies, Star Wars. Stuff like that. What's funny, is that some of that is closer to the truth than we really think about. But also, you guys ever look closely at a forest in the fall?"

Reggie, who seemed like the shyest one of the four said quickly, "Just walked through one yesterday. The leaves are all kinds of colors. It was so peaceful and beautiful, quiet, you know, but what's that got to do with what you're saying to us?"

Mag looked at Mark and V, who were smiling and then said to the four. "Well, I got an idea. We'll get Tim to pull that table along the wall over there and bring it around against ours. Oh, and if you want something more to drink or eat, we'll also have him take any orders for anything you feel like having. Then, maybe, I'd like, with the help of my two compatriots here, to explain ourselves to you which you might find it interesting. Whadda you say?"

Donnie grabbed Reggie and they huddled next to the girls. After a head-down discussion, he turned back to Mag and said, "Okay, we got a half hour before we gotta leave. So, we'll let you dudes tell us what's on your minds," he paused and said, "but frankly, we think you old dudes are nuts."

V replied, "Old duda girl here, my young dude. But you're right. Myself, and the dudes beside me are nuts, because we believe in something that controls us all…positively, not negatively like our world of these days."

Michelle, with pulled back dark hair tied in a knot, spoke up, "Okay, I get it, you three… believe, I guess is the only word, in some kind of world way beyond the Earth. Did I get it?"

V answered, "You did," then paused and added, "We just think humanity, us, is just an amazing creation of this Universe we are in. We think also that everything in this Universe, thus Earth, where we are, has a beginning and an end. We exist and then we don't, just like everything created in this Universe."

Michelle looked at V and then at her friends. She turned and looked right at V with her large dark eyes wide open and said, "You know, I'd like to talk to you all about what you just said."

CHAPTER TWENTY-NINE

As it turned out, they talked through the half-hour time limit that the young folk had said they would need to go for classes. They stayed for hours. Tim had brought a table over and four stools for them to sit on. He pushed the table up against the one that was there and took some orders for snacks and drinks. The four young ones sat down across from the three old ones. At first, they just talked a bit about their school majors, where they grew up, and their activities. It was a mixture of topics but apparently positive because two of the young ones called to cancel meetings with teachers and the other two just didn't go to classes. They talked back and forth into the late afternoon and the time was filled with phenomenal and honest conversation, including personal fears and hopes for their futures – not only for they themselves, but also for their country and the world. Mag, V and Mark were astounded by the honesty and fears that coalesced amongst the young ones as they spoke quietly of their lives for hours. Each had deep-down fears they said they'd never talked with anyone about, just within themselves. Finally, it was quiet and the seven sat looking across at each other.

"Why now, to us?", V asked.

"What do you mean?", asked Donnie.

"Why have you all opened up today about your lives and the things that bother each of you?'", V asked as she looked across at each of them.

Donnie responded quickly, "Because you guys seem fair and really interested in us. At least that's the way I felt after listening to you."

Mag responded, "Kid, I hear you. When you're your age, as I was some years ago, I know what you're talking about. You sort of live a life within yourself because you don't think you can tell someone how you really feel about things. We're so glad you all felt you could tell us how your lives are going so far."

Donnie's looked at Mag and said, as a slight smile slowly came onto his face, "You know when I watched you guys bullshitting over here from the bar, I labeled you as old farts, you know?"

"We are and you four are young farts, you know?" V replied smartly.

Everyone laughed, some lightly, but Donnie was uproarious as he responded, "Whoa, where'd you come from lady?"

"Wouldn't you like to know," V replied with a smirk. Then she said, "But what you should know is that we are all alive and well, except for my new, old buddy over here," she pointed at Mark, "who's suffering a bit, but whose brain is way beyond all of yours combined on the subject of what all our lives are all about."

Michelle interjected, "What's that mean?"

Mark, who had been quiet and hadn't said much since the four young ones had joined them responded, "Well. let me answer that one," as he paused, straightened up and went on, "Okay, it means, I'm still recovering from an operation, but doing okay, but not concerned, because we all," he pointed at them and then V and Mag, "are just momentary bodies of humanity spending a few seconds of life on this planet spinning around and around that Sun we see most every day."

Michelle straightened up and responded, "You make it sound like our lives mean nothing?"

Mark quickly said "No, what it means is that our lives—yours, mine, are everything. From day one to this day, each life is unique, never one like us before, now, or later. We each are universally unique, never to be repeated. Each of us must make the most out of these minutes, hours, days, months, and years that we exist."

"Exist?", responded Louise. "Exist," she repeated, "you make it sound like our lives are…no different than an animal."

"In some ways it is no different," Mark responded. We are animals of a sort. We know and are learning about what goes on in our own minds, to some extent, but not in horses, gorillas, or our favorite pets, dogs. They have their own special mind set. But, also, your mind Louise is totally different than your three friends or ours. Each mind, each life, is completely different. Oh, physically, we all have bodies and brains, and we function somewhat alike, but none of us are the same."

Louise responded quickly, "Listening to you, as I am, you make me feel like I'm different from everybody."

For a second it was quiet, no responses, then Mark said, "Well, you are. Basic physical alikeness, but down deep within you, you are completely different from everyone alive today or who has ever lived." He paused and then added, "Okay, let's see something. What are each of you majoring in at school?"

The four looked at each other and then Louise turned to the three, looking seriously at them and said, "Well, as I said I'm in grad school for nursing, but am also thinking about switching into physical therapy, but my real love is the theater."

Michelle straightened up and said, "Yeah, well, I'm not sure yet. As I said, I'm now also in a Health Care major to be a nurse but have thought about switching to be a doctor in internal medicine," as she paused then added, "but I'm thinking also about a degree in public welfare."

"Public welfare," replied V. "Could you explain what that means?"

"Helping poor people get assistance, like food, housing, and job placements."

"Wow, now that is worthwhile, for sure," V said as she looked over at the two young men who were quiet and said, "Okay you two?"

Donnie turned toward Reggie who sat next to him and bumped his arm. Reggie looked at Donnie, then across to the three older folks. Then softly he said, "When I was a kid, I wanted to be a pilot. Played with jets when I was a kid and in high school I flew auto pilots, you know the ones you can fly in the sky. But my grades weren't very good, so now I'm not sure what I want to do, except I would like to become a lawyer like my dad was before he passed away. So, I'm changing my program at Pitt to hopefully get into law school next year."

Mark looked over at Donnie who was sitting off to the side and said, "Okay, buster, let's hear your story."

Donnie looked at him and smiled as he said, "How much time you got, mister?"

Mark smiled and quickly replied, "Actually, probably not much, but my compatriots here have a lot. So, let's hear it."

The group of seven, all sitting around the two tables, now together, were quiet as Donnie shrugged his narrow shoulders and slowly began to speak.

"Okay, here goes. Got to tell you all my growing up days first because it has guided me into what I want to do with my life. So, hang in there. Guess I was about fourteen when my dad died. My mom had died a couple years before from a drug overdose and it about killed my dad. He was a very quiet, tough man who was a bit rough on me. He had worked for the Port Authority fixing streetcars which he'd done for thirty years when he died. When he died, he was in his fifties, so I went to live with my aunt who had been married a couple times and the guy I moved in with, was a real asshole. Anyway, I was really screwed up for a couple years, but for some reason, because all that had happened, I knew I had to get out of that house and the only way was to get good grades and go to a community college, especially in writing classes. I did so well in everything, especially creative writing, that I was able to get a scholarship to Pitt to study writing. As a kid and even in high school, mostly about some of the rough days and nights I had at home, I would write little poems and stories of what was going on around me. Somehow, a teacher at Pitt, who was on the scholarship program in their English Department read a couple of my stories I'd written that were published in a small publishing site on the internet and helped me get a scholarship. So, I entered Pitt three years ago and now I'm a Senior who will have a degree in Creative Writing from the Dietrich School of Arts. I…" he was interrupted by Mark.

"You are messing with us, aren't you?" Mark asked brusquely.

"No, why would I do that?" Donnie replied.

"I mean, for some reason… Oh, sorry, I just thought you were the bully of you four. I mean you're pretty good size and you seem to be the leader of this foursome, so…a writer? Sorry, it just didn't fit," Mark said.

"Well, it fits, whatever your name is, it fits," Donnie snapped.

"Mark, that's my name."

"Okay, Mark, I want to write for a living. In fact, I already have a book that a publisher is considering."

Louise interjected, "Donnie is telling you the truth, mister. I helped him put it together."

V interjected, "Hey, I'd want to read it."

"You're on, lady, for sure. Just happen to have a copy in my briefcase which is up at the bar. I'll get it for you," Donnie said as he turned to go get the notebook.

"What do you write about?" she asked before he could leave.

Donnie turned back to her and said, "Life in this screwed-up world for someone my age." Then got up and walked to the bar, picked up a briefcase and came back to the group, who watched him go and come back.

Mark said as Donnie sat back down, "You know young man, I owe you an apology. I call you young man because you are, and I am an old man. I'm impressed with what you just told us and also you others. I too, would like to read that book. Funny, our whole emphasis over the past days has been all about the same world you apparently have written about. I think we have more in common than you might think because I love to write poetry even in my old age."

Donnie was taken aback as he straightened up in his chair. He was silent for a few seconds and then said, "Okay, old man, maybe we could exchange our poetry. That would be great because I'm sure my world is different that you guys, but I can tell you what I was trying to write about in my book. That would be great."

Mag got into the conversation as he said, "Title, my man, what's the title?"

Donnie smiled and said, "Is That All There Is?"

No none said a word until Mark smiled and said, "Peggy Lee, I believe."

"Right on," Donnie smiled. "Peggy Lee. Now how would a kid like me, barely old enough to drink, know her and come up with a title like that?"

V interjected, "You heard the recording online?"

"Close", he replied then went on. "My stepfather, who did pound me a few times, wasn't a bad guy the more I knew him and he me, loved Peggy Lee, someone I never heard of. The music we have access today is wild compared to what she sang back in the old days, your days, I guess. Anyway, he played all her tunes on an online video site, and his favorite was that song. As I began to put down notes and ideas about what I wanted to write about, for some reason, that song, which I also could not forget, kept coming into my brain. Then as I thought about what I wanted to write about, namely: what is life for a young man in this screwed up society of this time, that song kept coming back. Then I realized that title is exactly my belief about what I see going on in this world of now, which I believe is on a short path to destruction. Can't see a way out," Donnie said.

"So, what's it all about, my young man?" asked Mag.

"Well, my man, as you say so well, it's about people my age and people your age," as he points to Mark, Mag, and V. "There is no connection, whatsoever."

"So, what does your book say?" Mag asks.

"Guns, killings, booze, dope, and on and on. This country is really screwed up and for us young people to understand a little about what to expect in the coming years is impossible. Money, money, money…period," Donnie replied.

Mark smiled and said, "Young man you are right on. Here's an example of what you just said or maybe it's in your book, which by the way I cannot wait to read for a couple reasons. We," as he pointed at Mag and V, "have been talking and working on, is about money. All the money I have created from the work I've done for almost fifty years. What the hell am I going to do with all this money sitting in a bank vault. Money, money, money…period, as you said so well. So, if you had it, what would you do with it?

Donnie looked a bit stunned as he looked to his

cohorts who were silent and unmoving. He then looked back at Mark and responded, "Well, I…we would try and figure out who would benefit most from it."

Mag tapped Mark's shoulder. Mark turned and nodded, "What's your take?"

Mag smiled a broad smile that lit up his whole face and reached out across his chair to grab Donnie's hand as he said, "Young man, I think you could join our team. In fact, I got a feeling all four of you could be our young contingent."

The four looked at each other and then back to the three across the table from them. No one spoke for seconds until V said, "What say we let you know our philosophy about life on this Earth and in this Universe of ours. I think you'll find it may be more in line with your beliefs than you think."

For the first time since they began their conversation a cell phone rang. Everybody at the table reached for their phones but the young four realized the ringtone wasn't theirs. Mag didn't have a phone and V kept her flip phone in her purse. Mark realized it was his phone, which he'd turned on to in case of any medical calls. He tapped it, then said, "Sorry folks, it's my doctor's office. Gotta take this one," as he slowly rose and walked away.

V said to the young ones, "He's got a serious medical situation and the doctor's call him a couple times a day to see how he is."

"What's wrong with him?" asked Michelle.

"He's got a problem with his pancreas. Serious, but hopefully fixable," V replied.

"I'm studying about that right now. That's a tough one to fix," Michelle quietly responded.

"It is. Not sure how he's really doing. He doesn't talk about it," V said.

"He is so calm," said Louise.

"Calm as a summer night," V responded.

"Is he a longtime friend?" Louise asked.

"No, but he has turned out to be my friend of life, you might say," V replied.

"That's quite a friend," Michelle quietly said.

"Can't be any longer than that, which is why we're here and why we're with you all," V replied.

Michelle smiled and said, "For some reason, I know."

Mark talked on his cell phone for quite a while, leaning against the back wall, away from their booth and tables. He turned and came back to the booth when he was finished, where, during the break with him on the phone, Tim had brought over a pile of sandwiches which the young ones were munching away on when he sat back down. He appeared strained and tense, as he looked across the table at the four eating away at their sandwiches and then back to V and Mag who were silent as they looked at him.

He smiled at them and said, "Well, it's not too bad. I have to go back in tomorrow. Something about a new assessment that they need to do. Some of my tests from last week came back and some adjustments need to be taken. We'll see, but overall, they thought I was doing very well."

Mag slowly replied, "That sounds okay, big guy. You ain't going to leave us early, are you?"

"Apparently not. This new treatment is getting some good reports at two other centers because they have reduced the cancerous portion in the pancreas. So, that's good news. I'm the fourth patient here in Pittsburgh on this trial, so it looks pretty good so far."

V smiled and said, "It's your attitude also, I think. You just don't give up, from what I have gathered over our days together."

Mark smiled, "My God, I found you two who appeared in my life out of nowhere and I'll be damned if I'm going to head to my universal sleeping place now. We got too much to do and now with our young friends across the table, I really want to see something beyond our little table world. Know what I mean?"

V and Mag nodded at the same time, and both exclaimed a combination of "I do," and "Right on," at the same time, which caused all three of them to laugh.

The young ones stopped their quartet of quiet conversation and munching sandwiches across the table. Donnie, with a sandwich half eaten in one hand said loudly, "Hey, what's up with you guys? Good news about the old dude?"

Mark barked at him, "Old dude, huh. I'll have you know, son, I ain't no old dude. A dude I am, but old, not yet!" causing them all to smile and let out hearty laughs.

V put up her hand and said, "Well, here we are. Now what? You guys heading out?" She paused and said, "It's pretty late for any classes."

The four looked at each other and Michelle said, "I know. We missed them all, but we can catch up. This was better anyway, at least for me."

"You want to do it again?" asked V.

"For sure," said Reggie, who had been the quiet

one.

"Sign me up too," added Donnie. "You guys are off the table, but you know, I think I got a book I can write about what you have been going on about the Universe and all that other stuff."

"Okay, then," V said strongly as she straightened up, "Let's have a get together tomorrow, later in the PM since our founder has a doctor's appt. Say around three P.M.?"

The four young ones stood up almost in unison and each voiced various approvals of the meeting time. They walked back to the bar as Mark, V, and Mag watched them.

Mark said, "Wow, I would have never believed I would have found such great kids in this screwed up country, in this screwed up time. They are terrific."

Mag smiled and said, "Gotta get me a couple of black youngins in here, folks. Balance, you know, balance."

Mark and V both nodded in agreement as V said, "Do that, Mag."

"I'll get on it. Got a question though?" Mag asked.

Mark asked, "What's that?"

Mag said, "What do I tell them? I mean what are we trying to create here?"

Mark replied, "Just tell them we're talking about a new world for everyone."

Mag smiled and answered, "Oh, yeh, that will get them, for sure."

V smiled and said, "Oh, damn it, I just realized I got two young single mothers coming in to the center after their work hours to talk about getting some financial help. They are suffering so much in their lives that what we have come up with, to me, is a perfect example of what we can do for those who need direction and help," she said as she got up and headed towards the door. "See you guys tomorrow".

"Well, it's time for me to get going Mag," Mark said, as he got up. Looking down at Mag he said, "Great day it was, and those young folks are going to make it for us," as also headed for the door.

Mag said, "Hey old man wait for me," as he got up and followed after him from the bar.

CHAPTER THIRTY

The group of seven were all there at a little after 3PM in the Bystander and Donnie was holding an iPad, as he sat between his three friends, who were sitting in their chairs across from Mark, Mag and V. Mark had asked him to go ahead and read the pages he had written after yesterday's meeting on a book he wanted to write.

Donnie looked at each of them and said, "First, thanks old folks for letting me read this. Okay, are you all ready for this?" No one responded so he looked at his iPad and began to read, "In twenty-four hours, the world changed, both on Earth itself and within the Bystander, my favorite bar. Outside the bar, countries may go to war. Outside the bar, guns may become restricted. Outside the bar, the two political parties in this country may be reduced by a new party. Outside the bar cell communications are frozen. Outside the bar the country and the earth are paralyzed. Inside the bar it's completely empty except for seven people, gathered around a table. Inside the bar it's dark because electricity has been shut off. Outside and inside the bar, life is at a standstill. The onrush of the instant breakdown of communication has created an electronic catastrophe never seen or felt before in the history of the planet. The world is dark when it is night and light only when it is day. Billions of people on Earth are stymied, from peasants to politicians. This has never happened before, at least as far as humans of this day believe," as Donnie paused and quietly said, "What do you think?" Then he added, "Oh, I think I'm adding a closed, silent bar as the center of the story. Does it seem okay?"

V replied instantly, "I love it."

Mag smiled as he reached across the table and tapped Donnie on his shoulder saying, "My man, that's terrific and I think you got something we can all help you with, if you want."

Donnie smiled, and said, "I do, yeah, I know I do."

Mark had got to the Bystander early and for the last hour he had been sitting back watching the group come together around the old round tables again and smiled at Donnie's obvious enthusiasm for using their discussions together as a theme for his new futuristic book which incredibly he had written since yesterday afternoon. After Donnie stopped and Mag and V had commented, he put his hand up like someone of his generation would do to get attention and they all quieted. Mark said quietly, "We need a theme folks and that is a great start, young man. One that captures our universal beliefs. So, lets…". His cell phone beeped, and he paused and said, "Sorry guys, I think it's my doc calling. Need a break, so keep working. But you all gotta know, that deep down in me, what we've accomplished together is so critical. But I gotta add something else and that is I cannot believe what has happened to me because of you all. I am incredibly at peace with myself for the first time…", as he paused again before adding, "ever." He stood up with his phone and walked to the back of the bar with his phone as he tapped in a number.

It was quiet for a few seconds as the four young ones looked at each other while Mag and V did the same. Then Donnie said, "I have known you folks for just hours, yet I feel I've known you for a long time," he said, looking at his three friends and then back at Mag and V. Then he added, "You know, you guys have inspired me writing my new book. For some reason, out of nowhere, I got a feeling, a sense, you could say, that our lives were supposed to jell. So, let's jell," and he laughed like he hadn't before with the group.

His three comrades also laughed to various degrees and slapped his back.

Mag replied quietly, "Jell it is."

At that moment Mark, in the back of the bar, shut his phone, put it in his pocket, walked back and sat down in his chair. The others noticed how solemn he looked and became quiet. Then Mark said, "I got to lay it on the line to you all."

The group all quieted and looked solemnly at Mark as he raised his right hand and said with a serious expression, "You got me for longer than you might want me." Then a broad smile spread across his face as he added, "The doc's said that everything they did seems to be working, so far it looks like I'll be around for a while with all you guys."

There was an eruption of cheers from everyone

at the tables, followed by V and Mag hugging each other and then encompassing Mark in a bear hug as the kids came over to hug them. The noise even caused the customers at the bar to turn and look over at them. It was chaos throughout the whole bar and Tim came around to them as they settled down.

"What the hell happened, guys?"

"The old dude has got a lot more time, Tim," Mag yelled.

"Fantastic, fantastic," Tim said as he came over and grabbed Mark's shoulder. "A shot of my best scotch for you, old timer."

Mark asked for Tim to lean over, and he whispered something to him. Tim stood up, smiled, and headed back to the bar, now busy with young customers. Over the next minutes, he didn't stop serving everyone at the bar, sometimes more than once. When he finally came back to the group of seven who were now centered around the table talking amongst themselves, obviously not talking philosophy, Tim tapped on the table. "Now it's your turn, you guys. Been pouring drinks like it's the last day on Earth, but now it's your turn."

"Wow, you are doing this for the whole bar, eh Tim?" said Mag.

"No, Mister Mag man, the big guy next to you is buying all the drinks for anyone alive inside this joint," said Tim with a broad grin. "Now it's your turn. Any of you want refills, give me a thumb up, okay?"

The four young one's raised their thumbs, but the three old one's did not. Tim walked over and took the glasses and mugs of the four young ones and said, "So, Mark, Mag and Veronica, you're, okay?"

Mark waved his hand, as did both Mag and V. Then Mark said, "Thanks, Tim, get me the bill after you do our young ones here. I think enough booze has flowed about; besides I think I'd better call my cabbie because I know its early, but I am whipped."

Mag responded, "Okay, what's the plan, now?"

V added, "Me, I gotta get back to the food center to help close it up."

Mark looked across at the four young ones and said, "Listen, I think we should reconvene tomorrow when you all are able to. Whadda you think?"

The four looked at each other, then conferred, before Donnie turned back to Mark and said, "We can be here around three, if that works with you guys?"

Mark looked at Mag, who gave a thumb's up, and V waved an okay. "Well, looks like it's a go for three P.M., right here. Does that work?"

The four all nodded their heads as they stood up.

Mark said, "Okay, all, three P.M. we go at it again. Let's all think about where we might go with our… theme, I guess is the right word. What can we achieve together to help those who need help in this one and only world of ours."

Mag interjected, "For your info, I may have a couple more to join our group, so we may need more chairs from our boy Tim."

V said, "Well, good, Mag, let's hope you do."

Mark added, "Great Mag," as he stood up and said, "Okay, my driver should be outside in a couple minutes and he doesn't like to wait, so see you all tomorrow. Oh, anyone need a ride?"

All raised their hands and Mark laughed, "Well,

I think we can do it. Let's go see Dominick. He's an old dude, like me, but he still likes to drive me around. I'm sure he can arrange seats for all of us in his cab."

CHAPTER THIRTY-ONE

Mark's appointment went very well the next morning, and the outlook was favorable. After a pizza lunch brought to him by his driver Dominick to Mt. Washington, he took a brief nap and was picked up by Dominick mid-afternoon. As he drove him to the Bystander, Dominick told him about dropping off the students yesterday and how he could hear them talking about how overwhelmed they were by what happened yesterday. It took less than twenty minutes to get to the Bystander as they pulled up outside at two-forty. Mark got out of his cab in front of The Bystander, waved as Dominick drove off and walked into what had become the headquarters.

As he entered, he laughed quietly to himself as he thought of some of the humongous offices he had entered during his career, and here he was walking into a hundred-year-old bar building, heading for a board of directors, which he now called his meetings with Mag and V. The place was empty, and he saw Tim down at the end of the old, oak bar tapping away at a computer that he had next to his cash register. Mark smiled as he walked down past the empty bar. It was close to three P.M., but he was the first board member to arrive.

"Tim, I'm here for a board meeting. Mind if I set up the board room?"

Tim looked at him with that huge smile of his, with a pencil between his lips. He took out the pencil and said, "Hello, boss man. You're early."

"No customers, Tim?"

"Oh, lunch was okay, but everyone's hit the bricks, but should pick up later," he said, turning, then added, "So, what can I get for you, old man?"

"Jesus, old man, already," Mark said as he walked past the bar and headed for the far corner where their office of two old wooden tables were just where they left them yesterday. He slid around and sat down where he had been seated the past days where he could see the bar and the front door. He smiled as though he was like a mafia don, who wanted to see newcomers coming into the bar. "Hey, Tim, I'll take some of that coffee you brew so well."

"Just made some, boss man. Give me a couple minutes."

Mark sat back and thought about what had happened over the past weeks, since finding out he had cancer. That just about took him down, but for some ungodly or maybe some godly reason, he had never felt more content with his life than right now, sitting in this chair in this dinky, old Pittsburgh bar. What had happened had been miraculous. And the two people he had become closer to than anyone he had met in his entire life was an occurrence that might also be described in some circles as miraculous. A woman in her fifties was like a sister he'd never had, and the black guy, built like a Steeler linebacker was like a son he'd never had. They had literally turned his life around; from thoughts of dying to overwhelming thoughts of fulfilling life. He rubbed his face and smiled as his eyes moved to the entrance as his black son came through the front door and headed his way.

He waved at Mag, who stopped to talk to Tim at the bar. Tim patted him on his arm and Mag continued walking toward Mark. "What's up, boss man," he said to Mark.

"Oh, no you don't, V and I gave you that title, big guy. You are the boss man," Mark countered.

Mag smiled and came over to the table, pulled out his chair and sat down. "Okay, V's, on her way. Saw her trucking down the street. Should be here in a minute or so."

"How'd your night and morning go, Mag?" Mark asked.

Mag replied, "Good. The Y is in good shape, and I slept like a log, as the old saying goes. Actually, I swam in the pool quite a bit, which I haven't done since I was in high school. Felt good and I could still move my legs pretty damn well. You ever swim much in all your exotic places around the world?"

"Did I ever? Maui was beautiful, but Puerto Rico, though, was my favorite," Mark said as he saw V coming down past the bar. He waved and said, "She's here. All we need now are the kids?"

Mag smiled as he said, "Oh, speaking of kids.

Got two coming a little later. Both go to Point Park downtown. The guy that runs the "Y" introduced them to me this morning. They were working out in the pool, which is close to school, so I talked to them about our little revolutionary group and believe it or not, they were both interested in at least listening to us."

V came up and patted Mark on the shoulder and went around to the other side of the table to sit down next to Mag. "Well, here we are again, guys."

Mark smiled and said, "That is for sure, V, but before the young ones get here, I've been thinking that we need to draw up a three-point plan for us. Something to cover our objective. You know, first clarify an objective, then how we are going to fulfill that objective and how do we use all that money I got stashed away to do one and two," then added, "That's just my thinking".

Mag looked at V and turned back to Mark, saying, "You know, this morning when I was talking to those two kids about coming here, deep down in my non-stop mind thoughts were saying to me, 'Boy, we need a plan so we can do something good in this world, especially with these young ones.' He stopped and looked at Mark, then V, and said, "We do have something working here when we both want to set up a plan. I'll bet you been thinking the same thing, V."

V smiled and slapped Mag on his shoulder as she said, "Got something right here, boys, right here in this notebook of mine. Whoever said it was right: 'Great minds do think alike,' or something like that."

"Wow, right on, V. We are all thinking about what's next," Mark said. He paused and said, "Well, maybe before our quartet arrives and Mag's new duo comes V, we can each go over our thoughts and see if there is any core similarity that we can use to begin to create our focus areas."

V says, "Great Mag. Young black kids, I take it?"

Mag responds, "You got it. A girl and a guy from Point Park. Musicians, yet."

V says, "Terrific. Okay, Mark, let's get going."

"Mag, you go first since me and V think you should be the leader of this crusade of ours, wherever that may lead us," Mark said.

"Well, okay, will do, if my lady friend nods at me," Mag responded.

V smiled and nodded at Mag, then said, "Well I made a couple man friends and that's worth everything to me. So, Mag old boy, go ahead, lay it on us."

Mag smiled and said "A leader I've never been Mark, but because of you and the V girl, my whole conception about what we call life, has for the first time made sense to me. I think I can lead us only with you guys helping me", as he paused and continued, "One thing for sure, I really believe we have come together and have never stopped thinking about what we've decided and let me just lay it on you." He pauses then says, "Okay, Mark, you have brought up two, maybe three, major objectives of our concepts," as he reached in his back pocket and pulled out a dark brown notebook, He opened it up and spread the pages then looked up. "No haiku Mark, but where I'm writing down my thoughts, so let me rattle off three things I put down which are what I believe to be our objectives, concepts, whatever you want to call them." He puts his finger on the notebook and reads, "One, our beliefs; two, Mark's millions; and three, a role for our organization in todays' world that combines one and two. We three have been discussing these topics over the past weeks and In doing so, the bottom line is to help folks have a chance to achieve their life objectives. One thought, which I think is terrific and unique in this screwed up world of ours, is to utilize Mark's method of seeking and settling disputes. We can start here in the 'Burgh by volunteering to help settle all kinds of disputes between local organizations; local companies; local political problems and maybe even like disputes between families and school boards. This would enable common, everyday disputes to be settled by folks we train, young and old, using Mark's methods. It would provide effective opportunities for folks, young and old, that would help them gain confidence in finding a career whether part-time towards their life's work or possibly full time based on their experience in dealing with disputes between people." Mag paused and then said, " I know this sounds like a pipedream, but there is something here that I think is just what we believe in," he pauses, "okay, that's me, that's my outline of what we're doing here," as he stopped then add, "What that means to me, is something we can do to help those without a chance in life," he pauses again and waves his hand, "Sorry one more thing", as he adds, "To tell you the truth maybe we can't do it all, but down deep inside me, I think we can," as he pauses says, "Okay, you two, your turn.

Mark and V are quiet. Mark looks over at V, then drops his head for a second, then looks up and over at Mag saying, "Stole some of my thoughts, of which I had five, maybe six, objectives, but you narrowed it down to a reality I think we can do. Frankly, though, you really nailed the most critical one, which is the reality of what we all believe in which is to give folks without much hope a chance. If we try to do too much, and it is just that, too much. If we have a specific objective, we can do it."

Mark turns and looks at Mag who says to V, "Whadda you think, lady leader?"

"Lady leader… like that," V replied, a wide smile across her face. She shrugged her shoulders and said, "The big guy nailed something as far as I'm concerned. Mine are similar, but specific, in that we latch on to one or two objectives as our trademark, so to speak. You know, we create a moniker that truthfully describes our beliefs so that when people see or hear our name, they know what our unique objectives to help people. Help people; my God, that is what we three believe in! Don't get me wrong, I'm not looking for an advertising scheme just to get attention. No, I want our name to be us, so that when we do something, whatever that might be, people will know exactly what we or our programs are designed to do. It will also make our young and old ones proud to be a part of what we're trying to do."

It was quiet as the three looked at each other, contemplating what each had said. Then Mark looked up and out to the bar. "Wow, this is hard for me to believe. This time with you two in my life. Then an operation to save my life. Then young kids who want to be with us, even me. I mean life can't be any better than what we have made it in such a short time." He paused and looked out towards the bar. "Well, I see those kids I was talking about are here, and I think there are two young

black one's behind them, Mag."
     Mag jumped up and headed towards the bar.

CHAPTER THIRTY-TWO

Mark could not believe what he was looking at on this late afternoon as he sat against the curved wall behind the wide wooden table with Mag on his left, and V on his right side. Across from them were six kids sitting in a curved setting on chairs. They had a variety of drinks in front of them, even a couple of draft beers for the two young guys, and different brands of pop for the others. In the middle of the octagonal table were several large bowls of pretzels, potato chips and a bowl of some kind of dip put there by Tim. The group was dipping and munching away as Mark raised his hand and the group got quiet.

Mark said to them, "Well, here we are. Nine souls; one old man, one middle-aged woman, one young dude and four young folks who we've spent some great time together. But now I'd like to introduce all of us again, for the two young folks who have joined us today thanks to Mag. First, there's the old guy, me, I'm Mark. Second, we have the next oldest one, V, the lovely lady next to me. Third, Mag, short for Magnificent, which he is, and he is the youngest of us three, but our new leader. Then we have our four students, including a novelist, Donnie; two young ladies now studying medicine, Louise and Michelle; and another young man Reggie, studying to become a lawyer. Lastly, our newest young guests sitting next to Donnie, invited by Mag, who are just starting college at Point Park and if it's okay with them, I'd like to them to tell us a little about themselves." He paused then said, "Okay, how about the young lady introduce herself for openers."

Mag leaned across the table and whispered to the young, narrow built, tan-skinned girl, who had a white Point Park University sweatshirt. She straightened up as Mag pulled away, looked around at everyone and said, "Well, I'm Ella, named after my granddad's favorite singer, Ella Fitzgerald, who is my idol. I sing too, but not like Ella," she paused and added, "wish I did, but my voice is more Broadway-ish, if that makes any sense. Oh, yeah, I'm Ella Brown and I'm majoring in theater at Point Park." She turned to the broad-shouldered young, dark-skinned boy sitting next to her.

The boy had a solid, wide build and was wearing a black jersey with Steelers in gold. He smiled and straightened up, then looked around at everyone and said, "Wow, this is quite a group of people, and I have no idea why I'm sitting here. My name is Oscar, believe it or not, because my grandad loved the piano player, Oscar Peterson. That's why Ella is my best friend because her grandad and my grandad played jazz for years together all over Pittsburgh. They named us after their favorite jazz players, and we've known each other since we were little kids. So, you all got a package when Mr. Mag asked us to come by today," he paused and added, "So, you have Ella and Oscar, Mr. Mag. How's that grab you?" he said with a smile, before adding, "You were so nice to us, Mr. Mag, so we are glad to be here. Oh, I'm also a theater major at Point Park and, pardon my sales routine, but we are doing a great play this winter, written by the great August Wilson, a Pittsburgh native, which you all should come to. He's a great playwright and I play a super role," he looked at Mag then and said, "Well, Mr. Mag, here we are," he said with a smile and took the hand of Ella next to him. They both smiled and lifted their arms together.

Mag broke out in his huge smile and said, "Welcome to our family, Ella, and Oscar, which I find hilarious, since I loved your namesakes when I was a kid. Gonna go to the play for sure. So glad we met up yesterday. I have a feeling you're going to fit right in with us and be a great part of this family we're building."

Mark brought his glasses up over his eyes and said, "Well, we're all in this tiny space, here in a bar of all places. We…" he paused, as a smile came over his face, "are a strange group, I must say, as I look at six young faces of different colors and then to my side, two older faces also of different colors. This is America for sure, of this day and age. I couldn't be prouder. So, if you all don't mind, I'd like to get us started in our session today by my reading a little poem based on the Japanese poetry of Haiku, which are poems in three lines that capture scenes of human existence better than any other writings there are, in my humble opinion. So, this tiny poem by me sort of captures, I hope, what us three, myself, Mag and V have created between ourselves. I'd like to read it to all of you to see if any of our beliefs we've been talking about make sense to the youth of this day, as it does for us older folks," he paused and added, "So here goes."

He took out his small leather notebook, leaned over and began to go through pages until he put his finger on a page, looked up and said, "Okay here is what I put down a few minutes ago, as I looked around at our tiny, yet magnificent group, no pun intended," as he looked at Mag with a wide smile.

Smiles crisscrossed the group as Mark put the notebook up in front of him and slowly read,

"Our Universe is endless,

Our lives within our Universe,

Moments of time!"

Mark paused and looked up at the young ones.

It was dead silent until V reached over and patted Mark's wrist, then turned to look at the young folks encircling them and said, "Incredible, Mark. It solidifies what you, Mag and I have been talking about the last days. So, let's continue by you folks telling us if those words have any meaning to you."

The four older kids and the two new ones just looked straight ahead for seconds, then Ella turned to Oscar and said quietly, "What's my momma gonna say if I tell her about what I think the old dude just said, leaving out God?"

While the four white kids turned towards her, Oscar reached over and took Ella's left hand, leaned into her, and said, "Well, been thinking what the man just said and you know, maybe God and this Universe are the same thing. You know what I mean?" He didn't realize that everyone had heard what she'd said to him along with his reply, which he'd said to assure Ella that he understood her.

Mag said, "You two young folks are right on because you both respected what my friend Mark expressed even though knowing that your parents or grandparents, those folks who mean so much to you and have their innate beliefs, might be disturbed by what he wrote," he paused and said, "No worry, Ella and Oscar, what we believe incorporates many beliefs, just in a different way."

It was quiet for a few seconds, then Donnie straightened up, looked over at his three partners on one side of him, then to the new duo sitting next to him, before looking over at Mark and saying, "You know since I first sat down and listened to you three, I have been playing with my new book idea which I told you about. It's made me think deep about what I want to do with my life, other than write stories, but what's funny, is that because of you three and listening to your little poem just now about, I guess you could use the word existence, it's got me thinking about writing something about life itself."

V interjected, "Life itself. Hmm, interesting, but I say you got it, young man. Life itself is what we humans call this…trip we take, from a crying, pooping eight pounds, to a crying, pooping hundred-ish pounds. Millions, billions of creatures that are created by various ways of insertion from one source into another, created somehow millions of years ago, into existences on this Earth. I know that is stupid, but we haven't got a clue as to why or how this was or is done. We are beings who see, talk, write, walk, create, live, die and yet, who have no idea who or what we are. All we know is that over the millions of years, somehow, materials were attracted to each other and eventually animals were created. I guess that is life itself as you just said," as she paused, dropped her head, looked up and added, "We aren't, then we are, then we aren't. That's it, but what is it?"

When V stopped, she looked at the young group sitting across from her who looked at her pensively without saying anything. They seemed frozen in thought until Reggie, who hardly ever talked, raised his hand.

V responded, "Reggie, you have something to say?"

Reggie replied, "If it's okay."

V responded with her wide smile, "Absolutely, please."

He straightened up with a serious look on his face and said, "My family is very religious and have been for generations. Me, I went to church since I was, oh, six or seven and still do. I've been taught that Heaven is where I'm going if I live a good life, so when I listen to you and your partners, at first, I thought you were bad people. Maybe people I really shouldn't be listening to, but my buddies here were all interested in anything new, as I really am, but wow, what you have been talking about seems to go against all I have ever believed. You know what I mean?"

V smiled and said, "I do. When I was a kid your age, I was rambunctious, a word of my time. I was that way, because I rebelled against my grandparents who raised me since my mom died very young and my father disappeared, sort of like what happened to my good friend next to me here," V paused and looked over at Mag. "I hated church, but strangely, as I got older and worked at various jobs over my years, primarily helping people, some very religious, I realized that people grasp at anything to explain and help them during this thing we call life. Pardon my English, but life ain't easy, young man and I hear you, and understand how you feel."

Mag said quickly, "Reggie, my grandma whipped my black ass so many times when I was young because I had the nerve to question her religious beliefs. You know, after what my new friends sitting beside me, and I have come up with in our talks over the past weeks is that God and religion may only be one way of recognizing the Universe. What do I mean? I mean that God is a name for an unknown, unseen power and maybe just a name for what we call the Universe. Okay, next thing, all the stuff about some dude name Christ going to heaven is a story of hope which people seek. Do I want to die? No way. Am I scared of dying? Yes. So back thousands of years ago, some real smart dudes said, "Okay, we'll give everyone some peace by saying, when you die you go somewhere by having just that…peace. So, you die and bingo, peace, except, I think, we just literally go to sleep forever, but without any more thoughts or fears or pains of living."

Reggie looked at his comrades and then his head bowed. He brought his hands up to his eyes. Tears were running down his cheeks. "Sorry, you all, I feel so sad."

Donnie reached over, put his arm over his shoulders, and pulled him next to him. It was quiet and then he said, "It's okay, buddy, I hear you and we're only talking here. We…and these folks don't know anything for sure. They and everyone are sort of guessing about life and what's after. Maybe nothing, but this is what they believe and maybe they're right but what I heard was that belief in God and Heaven, all that stuff, is maybe just another way of believing in what they have come up with," as he paused and added, "and they're not the only humans, I guess, who have a different belief system."

It was quiet for a few seconds and then Mark said, "You don't know…or you couldn't know how rewarding it is to listen to you all talk your truth. A word that is unused in our society these days because everyone is afraid to tell others their inner beliefs, whether their own or what they were taught. People say, 'Oh, yeah, I hear, ya,' but they don't. They just keep their inner belief to themselves so as not to differ with the other person. But what you just said so well, Reggie, is truth. One thing we must always honor is our belief system. It may differ from another person, but you can counter with, for example, 'I hear what you said and it's valid, it's good, but you know, I got a different angle which I believe ties in with your belief.' You don't disagree, you just offer your belief. If that person will not accept your belief, then you just subtlety back away and say something like, 'Nice day, isn't it?'

The group collectively chuckled softly, and Mag raised his hand, and they all got quiet as he waited for a few seconds and said, "You know, Mark, sometimes that is the hardest thing to do." He turned and looked right across at Reggie and said, "But listening to you, young man, I heard myself a bit because my momma and grand momma believed exactly the same way as your family. Nothing wrong with that. If you think about it, humanity is a species seeking answers about life; where it's been; what it is; and where it's going. Truthfully, no one knows. Thousands of years ago people created stories about the beginnings of humans with some realness and some unrealness if that's a word. Then, as humanity developed, some men became religious leaders and created beliefs to explain their version of humanity, its creation, its existence, and its end. Some of their beliefs were truthful from what they believed, and some were not, but they all tried to explain what human life was all about, our purpose and our end. But you know, not speaking for my colleagues, but goodness for your fellow man is a bulwark of my beliefs, because our time on this earth is very limited and our time afterwards is endless, one way or another."

Again, it stayed quiet, then Reggie said, "Sounds funny coming from me, but what you just said, Mag, makes just basic sense to me. I was crying just a few minutes ago, not from acknowledging what I grew up thinking, but from having second thoughts that would make my family mad at me," he was silent a moment and then added, "But you know, what you said Mag, and what I hear from your partners, doesn't nullify my beliefs from my upbringing, but just clarifies it. Heaven, whoa…maybe, may-not-be, but whatever peace you can have while alive, seems to me, would be heaven on earth, as an old saying my grandpa used to say to me. Now what he said makes not only common sense, but human sense."

In an instant reaction the others clapped, and Michelle hugged him, making him smile widely.

Mark put his hand up and they quieted a bit.

He waited a few seconds and then said, "Wow, we are on to something, for sure." He then looked away for a second, then back and said, "You know, I think it's time we pause for a few minutes to digest what we have just heard from Reggie and then concentrate on what we are doing sitting here as a group of nine. What brings us together, or I should say, what could bring us and keep us together?"

Quiet for a few seconds, then for the first time a hand went up from Ella, who had been sitting quietly beside Oscar while Reggie was talking to them. Mark said, "Oh, Ella, go ahead."

The young lady with wide, deep dark eyes straightened up and looked first at Oscar, then over to Reggie before saying, "When Oscar decided to come here, we had no idea what our new friend, Mr. Magnificent had in mind for us. At our age, we don't get much… what's the word I learned in my English Writing course yesterday, oh yeah, introspection, I think was the word. Yeah, introspection…introspection into how in our first years, we are usually channeled, another word from the class, channeled into a way of life. You know, school, maybe church, sports, if you have it available. Dates, if you really want to; summer job, if available; and college, if possible. She paused then went on, "Oh, I don't know, just everything your parents or parent, as in my case, wants you to do as you move into early adulthood. Adulthood, my word, but you know what I mean. Me, I have my music, my health, and don't need a boy to make my life for me, just the opposite. If I need to have a boy, it's going to be for good reasons, but now, all I want is to get through college and start creating a career in something I like to do and something where I can help people who need it," she paused, looked at Mark, Mag, and V, then left and right to the others, then said, "So, I know I was a bit upset earlier by what I thought my parents would be mad at me for listening to, but I know I'm of a different time than them. I love them so much, but I am myself, so I really liked what Reggie just said, and the others, so I think I'd like to stay around for a while." She turned to Oscar, "How 'bout you?"

Oscar smiled and gave a thumb's up before saying, "That Reggie guy was talking for me also and I'm with him and you all."

Mag straightened up and looked across at the young ones and said, "We've had some good thinking going on guys and gals for quite a while, but I think at least we need to take a pause and just talk to each other on anything that comes to mind."

Mark piped up and said, "Let's take a break and see what our chef has available for us. We can take a break and then maybe we can go on for another hour or so or meet tomorrow in the PM," as he paused, then added, " I think we should decide if this is just a get together and we go our separate ways, or can we all somehow come up with a plan to create something we all believe in; young, white, black, old, girl, boy, etc."

Donnie said, "Not speaking for us four, but I think we should work on creating some philosophy for us to follow as we, us young ones, go on with our lives."

Immediately, Louis, Michelle and Reggie nodded in agreement and Oscar leaned over to Ella to whisper. Then Ella looked up and said, "We're in."

Mag looked at them then to V and over to Mark before saying, "Wow, we're in the same groove. Look out world, here we come," which brought chuckles and laughter from the others.

CHAPTER THIRTY-THREE

It was an odd collection that gathered around the dark, wooden table off to the left of the bar in the Bystander. A collection of three older folks facing a mixed cross section of six young ones of mixed sexes and colors. The young ones were circled around a tall Donnie, who was tapping into his iPad rapidly, without stopping. None of the others were saying anything as they seemed entranced by what he was doing. Across the table, Mark, Mag, and V were all munching on various food items that Tim had brought over to all of them, but the young ones had devoured the miscellaneous food he had brought over in a matter of minutes. V lifted a roll of chipped ham that she had smothered with mustard and deftly fed herself.

Mag saw her devour the ham and began to laugh before saying, "Woman, you do know how to eat, I must say."

V smiled and grabbed another roll of chipped ham, smiled at Mag, and downed another as mustard lapped on to her upper lip.

Mag laughed and said, "You know how to do it," as he slapped a burger shut and took a huge bite himself.

Mark had been watching his two partners and said, "Wow, we have been working too hard. You guys must be starved," as he slid over a pile of French fries, picked up the ketchup bottle, and poured it. Looking at his colleagues, he took several narrow fries, drowned them in ketchup, leaned back and downed them in a second.

At that moment Tim came up and saw them working on his food and began to laugh, "Whoa, I know you guys love to talk and talk and talk but looks to me like you like to gobble food too. Sure, makes me feel good and I'll pass what I just saw off to my lovely spouse who came in to help me out in the kitchen. Molly will love this one."

Mag put down his burger and said, "My man, bring the chef-ess over here, we gotta thank her. It is good stuff."

Tim smiled and said, "I will when I can but for some reason this joint is jumping tonight, maybe thanks to you guys. The word must be out that the old man who bought drinks on the house was here so maybe that's why, thanks to the old guy, Mr. Mag Man."

"Mag Man," Mag replied, "you know, I like that. Mag Man, I'll take it. And give our thanks to her though."

Mark looked at Mag, then V, and said to them, "You know, I think it's time we get our little group together, either for a while tonight or tomorrow in the PM and decide a couple things. One, what do we do next with our philosophy of life, which I guess you could call it, with our group. Then, what I had talked to you about and what you said Mag earlier, as to how we can utilize all this money I have to do some good in this society of ours. Maybe using my work techniques isn't a bad idea, Mag."

Mag responded, "The more I think about it, I think it might work. Then I've been thinking a lot about these young folks across from us and how fascinating and interesting each of them is. Then I look up at the news over the bar, when he has it on, and read the papers at the library where I go when looking for what's going on in this country, I am overwhelmed by how screwed up this country has become. Look at those young ones. Pure, bright, and what kind of a future do they have when AK machine guns rule the country?"

V put her hand to her face and in a muffled voice said, "Funny you said that Mag, because I don't think this country is going to be around when these young ones are our age."

Mag looked away and then back to V saying, "Hope your wrong V, but know where you're coming from. You know if we do anything with our beliefs, maybe that's one thing we should concentrate on."

Mark interjected, "Name it, Mag, name it."

Mag replied, "Concentrate, that is the word, concentrate. We use the great mental folks I've read in the library. You know I guess you call them prophets. They believe that the only time in life is now; now, not before or after, but now…this moment is all that matters. Oh, I love to read about my brethren being hung and punished by white people back in the day or thinking ahead to computers controlling the world, but man," then he looked over at V and added, "woman, we should concentrate on right now. Now, now, this moment. You know what I mean?"

V chuckled, "Couldn't have said it better myself, and you know you got something for us and," she paused and looked over at their young comrades yapping away at whatever Donnie was showing them, "those young folks may have the answer to what we've been searching for. Now, right now, not before or after, now is what we can use as our theme. Help folks now; help ourselves, now; try and solve situations now that offend us or those young ones over there. Man, you nailed it, Mag."

Mark smiled and said, as he put his hands on Mag's shoulders, "My God, I just got through saying we need to come up with a plan and that's it, you two," he paused, looked over at the five kids and said, "and those kids over there will be our soldiers and compatriots."

Michelle, who'd been deeply in the huddle across the table, looked over and said to them, "Hey you three, wait 'til you listen to what Donnie has come up with."

V said back, "Wait 'til you hear what we came up with, but okay, Donnie lay it on us."

Donnie picked up his iPad and turned to them, "Whoo, it just poured out of me. You want to listen to me read it? It's just a first draft but covers what I think you guys are working on and what you were preaching to us. I think it's cool and frankly, opens up so much for me about what this whole thing we're in, that we call life, is all about."

Mag said, "Let's hear it now, my man, now." as he looked at V and then Mark with a wide smile.

CHAPTER THIRTY-FOUR

" "Uni-verse-soul' is the title and the story is about some young folks who take a trip to Canada and spend weeks by an isolated lake during their summer break. The goal is to come up with a new way of life for all the young kids in this old, screwed up world, pardon my language," Donnie said boldly, looking across at Mark, Mag, and V.

Mag said, "Cool, man, so cool. I think I got it. Uni, as in universal. Verse, like in poetry, and soul, like in…well you know what soul means, man, soul."

"Well, something like that," Donnie smiled his huge one.

V jumped in, "Universal…Uni…Verse…Soul… wow, Donnie, that is unreal. One poetic soul, that says it all. Because there isn't ever another soul like you, Donnie or me, or Mag, or Mark or anyone of our friends beside you. We are all absolutely unique; never before, never again, but now. Just like you were saying before, Mag, our lives are, the magic word, now, not before or after."

Oscar piped up, "So what about my family. What about their lives? I mean they were before…now. They go back a long time ago with me and for sure I'm living now, but I can't forget them now."

V responded, "Absolutely right, Oscar. But we're not, or at least I'm not, saying we ignore the past or think only about the future, but I am saying and believe we should gather from the past the best possible, positive things that happened. But we also need to recognize the worst things that happened and put them together into a package of understanding."

"What do you mean, ma'am? I don't get it," Oscar replied quickly.

V replied quickly, "Well, let me put it this way. You are young. Your family and personal history is short, compared to mine, for example. I mean I can go back over all that has happened to me over my fifty something years and list pluses and minuses galore, but what I can do and must do, is to sift out the negative reactions I took, or others did in my life that I recognize, so that in my now time and future time, I can follow the positive road and not repeat or go down the negative road," she paused and said, "Wow, hope that was clear. Make any sense Oscar?"

Oscar looked at her, smiled slowly and replied, "That was a lot, but I think I understand what you said because I've had both good and bad stuff myself in my life already, so I think I can grab on to the good or positive things and not the other."

Mag said, "Mind if I get into this, because as a chubby black kid in grade and high school, I have a feeling I know what you meant V and what Oscar is talking about. I think any kid, white or black or yellow or whatever, goes through that time. He's a kid, now a young man and in those early years, you are so responsive, no, that's the wrong word, so aware of people saying things about you for whatever reason. Kids are brutal to others, especially the weaker ones who need three or four others around them when they say shit to some solo kid. I heard it and finally, one day I responded with the punch of my lifetime. The so-called bully hit the floor and I was so happy. His gang disappeared, but back to Oscar. I don't know if you were bullied or just words were said that hurt you, but young man, looking and hearing you right now, you are on the right track. Accept what happened; what was said but toss it away. Grab on to all that you have accomplished. Grab it, hold on to it, and my young man, you will be okay."

Oscar smiled, "Thanks Mag, thanks. I get it and thanks. Will do."

It was quiet for a few seconds and then Mark said, "Well, that was so terrific. Gave me another idea for what we want to do with our, what do I call what we're doing…discussions, I guess. I have to say this, guys, and girls. You folks sitting across from us in our little corner away from the gang at the bar and my two partners beside me, have to come up with something for what we've been talking about together. At my age and with my medical situation, ironically, I have never been more excited about anything, than I am at this moment with us," he nodded to Mag and V and then at the six young folks sitting across from him and continued, "So, let this old dude get this off his chest. You guys over there do not know about me. Do not know that I am suffering from a pancreatic cancer situation and may not have to long to live this life of mine. It's better than I thought, and I may live for longer than I thought, but it's not certain. So, that's me and my medical problem. Mag and V and I have been talking for quite a while over the past weeks, right here, believe it or not, about the reality of life for us humans. It's positive stuff; reality versus superstition. I don't mean religion; I mean we have decided that religion is just a human version of hope for something in life and after life. It may be so, but what we have come to conclude, I think, is that what is absolutely critical and important is to concentrate on this moment, our now theory. Do your best at life, now, which V and you have just been discussing. So, you have heard us and are still here, so what I'm hoping is that you can grasp our beliefs and pursue it, explain it, and pass it on to your generations in the coming years in whatever way you can. Okay, I'll be done in a second, but also, I have been a very successful businessman in my prior life and have a lot of money. I want to have Mag and V, plus you guys, somehow come up with a plan to foster our belief system for young folks and even older folks, key word: somehow. Put our minds together now to help others now; for their lives now," he paused and added, "Whew, didn't think I could get that all out."

The group was quiet and then Mag said, "My Man you nailed it. That's our plan," as he looked at Mark, then V and then to the young ones sitting across from them. "Guys, you heard it. Got any thoughts?"

Donnie replied excited, "What Mark just said will be the plot of my book, Mr. Mag. Got to write it yet, but he gave me the plot," as he turned to his left and right, then back to Mark, Mag and V. He smiled and said, "Gotta say this. A lot of the social media crap and the often completely ego-oriented attitudes we talked about are going to ruin my generation. Somehow in this book, I have to use social media on some kind of absolute flooding method to get your, our powerful message out to my generation. We can't concentrate on just ourselves. We must grab the hands of others by helping and understanding. As a young one, I am scared that this country, which we don't even learn about anymore, is going to fall to some dictator-dominated country because our young folks just don't care as long as they have their cell phones to watch and listen to bullshit. Keep them fed and with clothes and their cell phones, they don't care who runs the country," as he paused and said, "Sorry, that's been building up since I read a letter my great grandpa wrote my great grandmother seventy years ago from Germany as World War II was ending," he paused again and said, "You know they don't even really cover World War II in schools anymore. It never happened, I guess the schools believe. Anyway, it got me. If we are going to really be a democracy that allows all people to have a chance at a secure, personal life, then we need to believe in what you guys are talking about. Know the past; realize there is a future; but concentrate on now, as you guys ironically have been preaching; this time, this moment. So, I got my work ahead of me and you all can help me get it done. Universal… 'Uni-Verse-Soul,' here I come," he said with a huge smile across his face.

It was quiet again. Then Mark straightened up

and said to the group, old and young, "We are going to create a miracle right here in this area which used to be the Steel Capital of the World. You will do it and I will help get you get started both with my business experience and the monies I have available from that experience. I am hoping each of you will become members of what I think can be a unique and helpful creation to provide leadership and objectives, especially for young people in this new world of the 2020's. I may not be here to see what we create, but I will know I had much to do with it being created for the benefit of people who need both protection and guidance in this new world.

CHAPTER THIRTY-FIVE

It's Spring, 2038 in Pittsburgh and baseball season is scheduled to begin tomorrow. Pittsburgh's Oakland neighborhood, the college capital of what was once called the Steel City is now called AI City, because four internet-developing companies, including two from Europe, moved their US operations to the riverside of the city. Tax free, but job oriented, the businesses raised not only the population of the once sparsely populated city, but also spurred a resurgence along the rivers for flourishing businesses and housing. Far from the maize of the East and West Coasts, it has both air and train connections that were upgraded and expanded dramatically in the past ten years.

In the Schenley Park, the beautiful park in the Oakland section of Pittsburgh, where world renown universities are located, a new glass and metal structure has been built, attached to the hillside that angles down to the ancient lake under the Schenley Bridge in Panther Hollow. It houses an international company dedicated to assisting students in gaining access to either colleges or companies that deal in what they call 'Universal Issues'. UniVerSoul Enterprises is the name of the company, and its corporate leaders are led by a large forty-eight-year-old black man named Magnificent Brown, who goes by Mag, and an older white woman at seventy, Veronica Angelo, who goes only by V. UniVerSoul has become both a national and international company well-versed in taking on controversial issues within governments, companies, and schools. It has also created a mediation program that has solved divisive issues amongst people of different nationalities, religions, and sexes.

The company started out simply helping advocates for students, parents and teachers in schools as well as helping schools settle disputes with local governments in Western Pennsylvania. After spreading to other States and eventually to helping neighboring countries with educational issues, UniVerSoul became world-renowned for settling disputes based on religious, political biases, plus corporate issues. Their motto is simple: Peace Versus Conflict. Even the United Nations has hired them to settle disputes of religion, borders, and water resources in countries, employing almost exclusively local people in their regional and international locations.

The founder, Mark Gentry, now deceased, started the company back in 2023 from an idea he'd had in a bar in the North Side of Pittsburgh. At that time, he suffered from pancreatic cancer which he fought off for the next five years at the inception of UniVerSoul, but it finally took his life. Mark, along with co-founders Mag and V, along with six young students at the time developed UniVerSoul, or UVS, the company's acronym.

The funds to create the company came from the millions of dollars Mark had gained during his long career as an internationally renowned mediator. His work had been based on his personal ability to bring two parties together and solve disputes that otherwise usually would have drastically and negatively affected both companies. He had a unique ability to 'cut to the chase', as he would say, to make the disputing sides understand that compromise was better than their mutual destruction almost assuredly in store for the companies if they couldn't come to an agreement.

Now, fifteen years later, the leader of UVS, Magnificent Brown or Mag, as he goes by, one of the three founders, is planning a meeting of the board in Pittsburgh along with Veronica Angelo or V, the third founder. The board is made up of them and ten others, including the six students who were with them when they started back in 2024, back when they were young college students and four corporate AI employees. Now, in 2038 the original six are living in all parts of the world, and one, Donnie, has been to the Moon as part of a satellite project which generated a best-selling novel.

All of the members of the board will be attending this particular meeting in person and will be arriving in town from their various international locations specifically for this meeting. The other four are financial folks who are stationed in Pittsburgh and whose role is to keep the Company operating with the company's latest AI systems, which now feature voiceless communication systems that keep them instantly in flow with all their programs associated with their mediation work.

Magnificent and Veronica had taken the structure

of Mark's business system and created their universal theme based on what he had created during his successful solo work agenda of the late 20th Century and into the current one. Mark had worked primarily with international corporations. UVS took the system he'd created and focused on designing first, a youth-oriented internet corporation that was designed to bond young people and educational/business enterprises, small and large, in Western Pennsylvania, and then over the years expanded across the US and throughout the world. Over the years they had ventured into all types of situations, some in small or large communities, worker/company disputes and settlements; and in 2038 their work has now become recognized nationally and internationally.

Mag and V were sitting in two lounge chairs in front of a window which looked down over the valley and a flowing creek below. Mag looked at V and said, "You know V, we should have our board meeting at our first headquarters. I mean we haven't been there for years, and Tim's still going full steam. He's got three kids and two of them are working at The Bystander. I popped in there last week and it was jammed. Tim was dressed up a bit and his oldest daughter was pouring beer. He must have fifty draft beers on tap with flavors I couldn't imagine tasting like the beer I drank way back in my military and goofball days, before I stopped."

V smiled and said, "That's a great idea. I'll get in touch with Tim and set it up there." She paused and said, "Mag, you know, everything these days is created by AI, even flavor favorites. Was thinking the other day how Mark, would be dealing with this 2038 world we electronically live in. Glad we're getting our gang together in person because the last years our board meetings have just been online because the way we're going, we need to come up with a program that we humans design and not our AI system that controls just about everything. Was thinking yesterday about the old man and laughed to myself because if he is tuning in to us and the world of these times, he would be raising his quiet voice and pointing at us to do just what you decided to do by having this board meeting. He would approve of us old folks and our now older young folks in the flesh, so to speak, meeting in person, like we used to for so many years. He would be so proud of how we have turned into a worldwide system of mediation based on what he created so many years ago. So, let's get on with it, 'old sport,' as one of my favorite characters in a book that no one these days ever heard or read about, The Great Gatsby, would say," V said.

"Never read it, 'course I never read anything when I was young, except sports articles…" Mag paused and then said, "Wow, you know V, we are getting old," he said with a wide smile.

V responded, "Old, yeah, for sure. Me, I got you by, what, almost twenty-five years, so maybe I got another ten in me, and you got another forty or fifty, so let's just do what we can to keep this sucker going. But I've been thinking we need to bring in a couple of our folks to begin getting involved in running our systems in person, here in our headquarters. The way it's taken off, we'll need them here, soon," V said.

Mag replied, "Glad you said that, because that's what I was planning to make the most critical thing we discuss at our meeting. I want to ask a couple of them to return to our online office set-up and begin to take over," then he thought for a moment before saying softly, "Actually V, I think I'm worn out. The last fifteen years have been unbelievable, but me, myself, and I, haven't had a life. Fortunately, I got my Maria, thanks to the Universe, and my two kids, but inside, I'm worn out. This thing has just taken off in this new universal atmosphere like nothing I imagined. Mark, I hope is tuning in, because he wouldn't believe how our little get-together in The Bystander between the three of us has created a phenomenal universal oriented life of working opportunities for a whole lot of young ones and now older ones. A couple things would really make him so happy, but one thing he did in his last year was really the catalyst. That was when he contacted that lady friend of his Marsha McDonough, who was his supplier for years of business conflicts. She got us handling health and educational related groups that needed a mediator. I'll never forget going to my first situation with Mark, who was not doing well. It was remarkable how he totally calmly and quietly controlled both sides and they left, shaking his hands and even mine. From then on, Mark and our group handled our meetings so well, that we got all kinds of new business in the following years, even after Mark passed on. Ironically, our group began to get referrals that weren't typical of what he did during his career. Until she passed on, Marsha for a few years after Mark passed away replaced him as our elder provider of new business. Mark would be astounded by how we used his tried-and-true methods of bringing opposites together to form a unified objective on some of the projects she found for us and ones that began to come to us because of our great publicity."

V responded, "Oh, yeah, Marsha was something else. I think she had a crush on Mark, but he didn't know, I'm sure." After a moment she continued, "Oh, and since we're thinking about those who helped us because of Mark, how can we forget that strange old CIA dude, Trevor. He told me once that he knew Mark hated him, but he thought Mark was a genius. They grew up together and he ended up giving us about five legitimate contacts in D.C. that needed some help negotiating Federal projects and local communities. I couldn't believe how difficult those were in comparison with some of the questionable internationals we got involved with who knew exactly what they could and couldn't accept. But we still settled many government and public situations. Not like what Mark did, but still smaller contract disputes that we settled. Yeah, old Trevor, who died, what about five years ago, was something else and the irony is that Mark never knew that this once big-time dude in the CIA really respected him."

Mag smiled as he said, "Mark was the most unselfish person I have ever known. He never took what he did for a living or what he had created with us as some mark of distinction for himself. And I know what would make him ecstatic would be how many of the young ones with difficult upbringing situations, but who had personal gifts of potential achievement navigated themselves into terrific work situations in this AI world and with us. He would be so thrilled and so proud," Mag said as he grabbed hold of V's hand and squeezed it tightly.

V replied, "As you were talking and we were

remembering some of his old friends, we can't forget Sol Weinberg, his old Army buddy who beat Uber by fifty years. His estate gave us over four million big ones for scholarships which we are still doling out. I mean Mark had only a few friends, but they were just that, friends, even after his death. You know I was thinking earlier today about how his hometown has become so involved in this new AI world. Now Pittsburgh in 2038 is right in the middle of this human revolution."

Mag chuckled and replied, "It reminds me of a book I read a couple of years ago about Pittsburgh in the year 2050. In fact, that was the name of the book: 2050. Ironically, some of the things in the book have come true and here we are doing what we are doing across the States, and now into the world, from the Pittsburgh of 2038."

"Never read that book, but I might remember seeing you with it," V responded.

"Well, it was a good read about an America breaking up and look what's happening V," Mag paused then said, "we're living in a divided country. East Coast; West Coast; country states in between; and big cities versus rural communities. So divided, plus social media that took over twenty some years ago along with AI created a country filled now with so many young ones of that time now in their forties, who only want what they want, if you know what I mean. We got some old school ones like us and the younger folks working with us, who, thanks to Mark, sort of live by old school motivations of work, don't shirk, a line Mark through at me many times. So, our younger folks need to keep pouring it on to folks their age to yes, succeed in their lives, but they also must protect and help their fellow man and women, for that matter. 'Life ain't easy,' my mom used to preach to me, and she is still right", Mag said.

"Well, we've finally lost our two-party system, thank God. We were really in trouble back in the days when we got started and what we did to help get rid of it," V said.

Mag replied, "Mark sort of got us started working on a multi-party system like Europe. He would love that how we helped bring political people together who differed so much, we weren't sure they would stay in front of the camera together. However, millions watched on their sites, and it worked. The voters came through and we have our new European political model of five political parties that has worked which might be what will save our country. We are close to 350 million people of a different mix of whites, blacks, Latin's, Orientals and whatever else, but I think we still must maintain some of our basic beliefs. Most of our negative issues have been addressed—look at me, for example. And whose running this country now: women, blacks, and Hispanics. It's a new world with more balance between the countries than it used to be, mostly because everyone is aware of what the other is up to because of AI. There aren't too many secrets in the world, of these days, that's for sure, which is why I want to talk about just that to our folks."

V didn't reply immediately, as she usually did. Instead, she looked out the window and down to the creek flowing below for a few seconds before replying, "You're so right, because it's getting better, I think, because we are all so entangled with AI that everybody knows what everybody is thinking, planning, or doing. But you're right, maybe we'd better go back and talk to the big guy, Mark. I mean let's just stop for a second and think how we would talk with him about what you just said, which I entirely believe has become a problem in this AI world. What would he say and do if he were alive and, in our shoes today."

Mag ran his right hand over his face as a smile came and quietly, he said, "Wow, you're right, what would my man Mark say to us right now about what's going on." He thought for a moment before adding, "Oh, I know he would be so proud of all that we and our young ones have done over the past years, but what he would say about the U.S.A of 2038. I would be afraid to ask which gets me to something I've been thinking about over the last weeks."

V responded, "What's that?"

Mag looked out the glass towards the valley and creek down below, then turned to Mag and said, "I think our next project has to be about the product that has led us into our successes over the years, AI."

V said, "What about it?"

Mag replied, "I think we have to join up with the folks at Carnegie Mellon and the University of Pittsburgh's AI systems and jointly work on making sure that AI does not go on its own over the coming years. As much as there is to fear about human beings trying to use it negatively, we should somehow make sure that the AI systems don't also. Know what I mean?"

V sighed and said, "Been thinking about the same thing and I think we should bring it up with our team, today."

Mag sighed and said, "So glad you said that, and I will."

V looked at her watch and said, "We'd better set up our meeting and let them know we're meeting at the Bystander who I will contact and set up. I think what you just said is a super idea. Their coming from all over this world, so it will take them a day or so to get here so we got so much to cover."

Mag stood up and said, "Let's get on it."

CHAPTER THIRTY-SIX

Tim could not believe what he was looking at from the kitchen door at the end of the bar. The bar itself, as usual, was not crowded as it was early for the lunchtime crowd that he always got, but behind the end of the bar against the wall, was something he had not seen in years. A mixed group of folks of all colors, ages, sex, and attire were all sitting quietly listening to his old friend from many years ago, the magnificent Mag. Mag was in a dark blue sweatshirt with a hood lying behind his head as he pointed at a large movie screen set up on the wall. Tim walked up behind the group of the younger partners, stopped, and listened.

Mag spoke, "It's been a while since we have been all together in our headquarters," which caused laughter from the group. He then said, "That caused a laugh as it should, but people would laugh if I told them that our great organization was founded in the Bystander bar in Pittsburgh. We know differently. We know that we came together almost fifteen years ago because we realized that our world of that time, though different, was at risk by overwhelming negativity flowing through our systems of communication. People were becoming controlled by AI, so our founder, he would not like that title I know, but anyway, Mark Gentry in his career had garnered over 25 million dollars that sat in a Zurich, Switzerland bank and he allocated it all to creating our organization. What was its purpose? Its purpose was to use those funds for his idea of bringing people together who differed. Who were they? Well, over our 15 years it has been politicians, school boards, companies, governments, people of alternative genders and sexualities, gun owners, immigrants, and many other opponents, who were brought together, not by the internet or the virtual crap, pardon my expression, but in person collaborations with all of us and opposing interests. Opposing groups would be represented in person, in the same room, and be sitting across from their opponent at a table, with one or more of us moderating them to agreements. Yes, our world has become overwhelmed by the consistent tap…tap…tap way to communicate and then AI even used people's eyes for ID. But, even with the elimination of people talking to people, we retained Mark's old-fashioned methodology of 'in a room,' as he used to say, 'person-to-person.' So…" Mag paused, then said, "enough of me. It's time for each of you to tell us all what you are doing personally and with us. Let's start with our worldwide acclaimed writer and Moon man, Donnie."

Donnie sat in the middle of the six curled around the same table as years ago. He looked to his left, then right at his longtime friends, then across the table at Mag and V. Smiling, he said, "Wow, I cannot believe this corner is still here, and the same as it was. We spent so much incredible time here talking about everything, and I mean everything. What's funny is that my second book, which became popular, was based on all that we covered in our back-and-forth conversations. Many books have followed, including the one about my trip up there," as he pointed towards the ceiling and continued, "which I dedicated to Mark for what he did for me. It was exciting for sure, but what was funny as I walked on the Moon, I looked at Earth and realized how much we, us, had done to make it a better place for us humans. It was exciting and a bit weird, but I'd go back just to be able to look at our spiraling Earth," as he paused and wiped tears from his eyes. "Sorry, being here and remembering how I was when I first sat there," as he pointed to a chair across from Mag and V, "I cannot express how much what Mark and you two, plus my buddies who were with me when we started have done for my life." He paused, cleared his throat, and added, "Okay, an update on my writing which also really started here. Now I'm working on a streamer that will be a bit historical in that I use our group back then as the catalyst for the story. So, okay, enough about me, but I can't believe I'm back here at this table."

Mag responded, "So glad you're at this table, as I am. Okay now, how about Michelle."

Michelle stood and began, "I'm married to a teacher, have two kids, and work at the University Hospital as a doctor of internal medicine after I switched out of nursing. Fortunately, over the years I have traveled to

Africa many times and set up several medical clinics in poverty-stricken areas. The University supported my extra work overseas and eventually allowed me to concentrate on representing the University in my endeavors in Africa, which was a first for them. I also began to utilize my training with UVS by bringing together three African governments medical services with the help of UN and US representatives to coordinate proper medical facilities for families who had none. I helped organize the three countries in the transfer of funds to pay for these medical services. Each country was initially against receiving outside help. However, when African citizens of their respective countries, who were taught by UVS, came together, they were able to reach agreements on overseeing the funding. This was done to prevent the usual case of funds being stolen by government and native leaders in many African countries. The successful health improvements of the citizens, along with a drop in births due to proper birth control medications and pills, stabilized the outrageous birth rates of poor women by hit-and-run men. Women were now becoming stronger and more independent throughout Africa and thanks to what UVS did for them. I cannot speak more positive about what has been accomplished by UVS and I want to thank Mag and V for their support over the years." She paused and added, "Just couldn't wait to get here to thank you in person," she said, as she sat back down.

V responded, "You are such a symbol of what we talked about those many years ago. Thank you from Mag and me and of course our guy, Mark," she paused and said "Okay, how about Louise."

"Just three words from me. Thank you, guys,"

Louise responded quickly as she stayed seated.

"That's all, Louise?" V responded.

"Well okay," as she stood. "I'm still single. As you all know I finished my nursing career but switched into physical therapy which I love. I'm in New York with a terrific group doing physical therapy for many people but concentrating on low-income folks who have not been able to get PT in past years. I really love doing my work because I help so many people, but I also spend much of my vacation time going out West helping three Native American Tribes. I do this because of your help, plus our beloved Mark of those years ago."

"Wow," V said, turning to Mag whose smile lit up his face. "Well, okay, let's move on to Reggie, our barrister, eh?"

Reggie who was the quiet one years ago, straightened up and said, "Well, my life has been a roller coaster and being here is certainly at the top, like my rides at Kennywood Park in my young days. What a ride it has been. I was in my grandparents' hometown, a small town in Estonia, for three months, not long ago. It has recently become a separate country again from Russia, which as you know, retook it ten years ago. The government, which has been recently reformed and is attempting democracy again, needed legal help with the United Nations which I provided. I got the government; powerful company owners; individual citizens; and UN leaders together in Tallinn, the capital. Wow, what a beautiful old city. It was incredible," as he paused and said, I know I'm going to go over my time, but I must tell you, what UVS did was incredible. The folks in Estonia were all angry people; each segment hated the other; each segment wanted their plan to put in place. And me, I just listened to them going back and forth until finally I put my hand up and said, "UVS will incorporate a portion of what each of you wants, so tell me your most important thing you want in this new government. It was quiet and then in the next ten minutes…only, believe me, they fumbled around first, but each eventually came up with their own critical need which led them to come up with a policy for the new government. Oddly, several were similar, but in less than an hour, they all buckled down and agreed on a major philosophy for Estonia. I could not believe it, nor could they. Now Estonia is stable and on a terrific path of freedom and stability thanks to our old beloved boss, Mark, and you guys across the table."

It was quiet for a few seconds and then they all clapped their hands, as Mag and V hugged. Then Mag let V go, turned, and said, "Incredible. Absolutely incredible." He looked up at the ceiling and said, "Mark, my man, did you hear that? I know you did." It was quiet again and then he said, "Okay, almost done. How about the deadly duo at the magical keyboard, Oscar, and Ella?"

The seriousness broke up a bit and there was clapping as Ella said, "Me, this little girl from Homewood who works for the State of Pennsylvania in health care, just got in from setting up a meeting in a month in D.C. My experience with the State helped me set up this meeting between the AI Symposium and our Federal Government, which will spend two weeks working together to combine all federal assistance programs for those under $125,000 of pure working income and government assistance. Congress must approve, but there were members from all the parties there. As we, and many States, helped the Fed's to combine Medicare and Medicaid into one program five years ago into Personal Care or PCP, all the miscellaneous programs still floating around within Federal and State programs will be processed and put into an individual Federal program," she hesitated, then added, "From what I heard this all happened because Donnie Boy wanted a beer fifteen years ago." Laughter erupted again as Ella patted Oscar on his back and said, "Okay, your turn."

Oscar smiled, straightened up his narrow shoulders and responded, "Okay Ella, mine is easy. As you all must know, I do play the piano, not as good as the one and only Oscar, but pretty damn well. About ten years ago I was playing in Morgantown when a young girl asked me if I could come to her school and listen to their quartet, which I did. Anyway, the quartet was two young black kids and two young white kids. They were terrific. Anyway, over time, I mean two years, I got them scholarships to four different schools and guess what, each of them still play their instruments while finishing college and have jobs and two have families. It got me thinking, and in the past five years I formed a collaboration with music organizations here in Pennsylvania, West Virginia, and Maryland and now around the country. We seek out players from schools, and schools who have kids looking for places to get degrees in music, and jobs in businesses looking for musicians. A crazy idea, I know, and in many cases over the years some of the kids even went overseas, but it was UVS that helped me get schools and companies in the same room to come together and hire these kids."

Mag looked at V then to the circle of associates in front of him and said, "Well, guys and gals, it's time to jam a bit about what we, UVS, does next and I have some phenomenal news and a new project which I need to share with you." Mag then stood and looked across to the collection of younger folks, who were now silent looking at him. He looked down at V and then back out to them and said with that huge smile of his, "It is an incredible feeling standing here in our headquarters where we got started and looking at you all. It is a bit overwhelming, but I want to start with some incredible news for us all. Listen closely, like we used to listen to Mark. Today, UVS, will be named by the United Nations as the number one organization in the world for bringing people of different beliefs, needs, nationalities, and goals together. The UN has also created a special committee to design a new unit operated by UVS within their organization to inform countries around the world to set-up problem-solving meetings between opposing sides, whether it be financial, business, or political," he paused and said, "So you all here did this and we all know how proud our Mark is as he no doubt is watching l us." It was silent for a few seconds and then a thunderous applause broke out, yelling and hands raised in the air. When it quieted down, Mag reached over to a now standing V and patted her shoulder and said, "V, some words, please."

V remained standing as Mag sat down, while the younger ones looked at each other then back up to the gray-haired woman, who had proved to them over the years that she had an incredible mind. Over the years she'd had many discussions with them separately and as a group. She spent time helping them to make decisions, much like their own methodology of solving problems for others by weighing pros and cons. She always cut to the chase, outlining what the end result must be to settle differences. So, as she stood there after Mag's announcement, they all patiently and excitedly awaited her perspective.

V looked out over them, smiled, and said, "Okay, our boss, I know, is smiling wherever he is. He can't, I can't, and I know our buddy boy beside me cannot believe what he just said. We started out right here in these same chairs in this old Pittsburgh bar. Who in the hell in this world would believe all you have done in this world from our beginning? No government, not even the United Nations, could see the value of Mark's philosophy of solving problems, but we bought into it and have created a way that people can solve difficult problems. We call it mediating, I call it reality. There was a President many years ago in the U.S. named Ronald Reagan, who was, excuse the expression in this day and age…no, forget what I just said. He was a Conservative. Okay, maybe I'm a Liberal; compared to him I guess I would be, but this President made the comment after getting a result dealing with members of Congress who were Liberals that getting 80% of something was better than getting 100% of nothing. It was something like that, but what he meant was that by talking and negotiating with the opposition, he got a lot of what he wanted, and they got some of what they wanted. Now maybe he got more than our folks get because we sometimes have sides settle for half of what they want, but at least they have that instead of zero. So, what I am trying to say to you all, is that what Mark did all his life, and passed on to us and to so many in this world, is that talking with the opposition and settling disputes is better than leaving problems and situations either unsettled, or causing a battle that helps no one, except maybe the stronger of the two in some way. This philosophy that you all have promoted in so many places, now even in other countries, has caused our world to take a deep breath and has created peaceful resolutions to difficult problems instead of continual battles," as she paused and said, "Well that's my two cents worth as we used to say many years ago, but it's the best two cent value ever."

Mag stood and patted V on her back and said, "Wow, that was right on, as I used to say years ago. You nailed it, V." After a few seconds he said, "Okay now something has come up that I need to present to you. V and I both agree on this proposal. So let me spell it out and get your opinion," as he paused, reached down, and took a sip of water. He straightened up and said, "This involves AI. AI has been our bread and butter in interacting with organizations and systems around the world. We use it, the world uses it, but V and I are concerned that maybe we must put a group together, internationally, that will try and make sure that AI components do not begin to act independently of human control.

CHAPTER THIRTY-SEVEN

It was a revolution that Mark, Mag, and V started, but instead of a negative one which brought violent warfare to overwhelm a government and put in a new one, it was a universal achievement that brought people together. The bottom-line for the original force that began with simple, personal handling of opposite views had blossomed into a national, then international, method of solving and soothing disputes. Solving and soothing became one of Mag's lines, of course, and school districts, townships, libraries, union workers, along with a slew of local peoples found solutions for disputes. In the world of 2023 when Mark sat in the bar and Mag came in, followed later by V, the country and the world was in total chaos with divisive and destructive ways of life. Guns were killing people; cars were killing people; and the country was divided into two beliefs; one, ultra-liberal and one ultra-conservative, yet they accounted for only fifty percent of the population as the other fifty percent were neutral politically. It took four national elections to resolve the political mess that existed in 2023, when Mark, Mag and V began their system. In the following elections, gradually the fifty percent of Independents grew into a solid political segment and party, which divided the country into three parties instead of two which eventually led to a multi-party government system.

The President in 2032 was an Independent who touted Mark's belief system that had earned national recognition for solving all kinds of local and national disputes. She spoke of Mark, who had died, and his philosophy when she sat down with two other candidates and covered every issue of that time. All three did very well in the three public debates held on social media and the national networks, but she was outstanding. Nicola McDonald from Nebraska became President of the United States, with LeRoy Brown of Georgia as her Vice-President, with the Unity Party. Congress was now divided between three parties, with several other parties also having some percentage of Congress. No party held majorities and they all had to work together to resolve issues. It was somewhat like the political structure in Europe, and it was and is a success as several of the other parties had become national. All because a man from Pittsburgh got cancer, met a down-in-his-luck black guy and a fifty-five-year-old woman whose life was built around helping people out of hard times in their lives.

It was now 2038 and Mark, the founder of what is now called UVS, had died ten years ago. Mag, now forty-eight, and V, close to seventy, were now the dual leaders of UVS, and they sat at the wooden table in their original headquarters in the Bystander Bar in

Pittsburgh. across from each other the Oakland area of Pittsburgh. It was break time for their meeting with the original group that started their company.

Mag looked out towards the bar where he could see the younger folks gathered together and he turned to V and said, "Well the others will be back shortly from the break, do you mind if I go back fifteen years to when this all began for us. Then we can set up our agenda for handling AI and I'm going to ask Donnie and Louise, if they will work with us here in Pittsburgh, say monthly at least and also via satellite over the next year to create our position on monitoring AI, along with input from the others. Does that work for you, V?

V smiled and said, "Go ahead. If they accept, I know the others will add some great stuff because their involved in so many different AI areas. So, I totally agree with choosing them and I know the others will be with them. She laid her wide smile on Mag and as she reached out and took ahold of his wrist. "Go ahead, big guy."

Mag returned the smile and said, "Well, I remember the first time Mark said his favorite belief, 'Each day is a life' that he believed was what life was all about. He was so right. I mean, I know we and I'll bet all those folks out there," as he pointed to the bar, "follow that motto. One must try each day to fulfill their life's purpose. Mark would talk a lot about how so many humans worked 18 hours a day and slept 6. That we work in the daylight and sleep in the dark, except for those who must work at night, like cops. Remember, he would go on and say to us, 'trivial, right?', and at first, when he would say that we would nod our heads because we had no idea what he was talking about. I remember that he finally got through to us that our lives are short, as far as the Universe is concerned, but that in that short life span of say, seventy, eighty years, if your fortunate, one must realize that every minute, hour, and day is super critical to you fulfilling all that your brain and body were created for. I remember that I finally got it. I think of just that line many times. Mark thoroughly believed that human life was a natural creation of the Universe. Remember V, how he would say to us, 'While the Sun shines on this tiny planet, each human has a moment of existence.' Then go on to say that existence is a Universal rarity; that our minds and bodies are a rarity; the time we exist is a rarity; but it is real because we were created by the Universe. I mean he told us once that over his fifty years of working, the reason he never married and had children was because he spent his entire spare time seeking information on the Universe and following our space program intensely which is so ironic that one of his young folks, Donnie actually went to the Moon. He would be or is ecstatic about that. So, to Mark a day in life was Universally unique, so we should live it to its fullest, which he did, for sure." Mag paused, rubbed his chin, smiled, and looked at V, who just looked at him solemnly, then smiled and said, "Each day is a life, wow, he really nailed it".

V finally responded, "Whew, you really captured him, Mag," as she paused and said, "I remembered him telling me one day when you were somewhere in the restaurant, 'V, this was meant to be, you, Mag, and me. The Universe brought us together in some way, I really believe that.'" V's head dropped, then came up and she added, "You know, looking back at what has happened,

I now know what he meant, and he was right.”

The others had come back silently and had listened to Mag and V reminisce. Then Donnie said, “Each day is a life. Is that what he said to you?”

“Oh, yeah,” Mag replied. “He said that many times and felt it represented how critical it was to do just that; do the best you can each day of your life. He felt that our lives were unique and precious in the Universe, especially if you, we, were healthy and able to compete in our living world, which we are, fortunately.

“Well, that’s a book, for sure,” Donnie replied.

“I’ve read your novels, Donnie. I can’t wait for you to take this concept of Mark’s and create a story somehow that would combine his beliefs,” Mag said.

“There is a story there for sure, and what makes me excited is that what he talked to all of us about those many years ago and what we’ve all achieved using his philosophy is for sure a story to be told. Hopefully, I hope I can do it,” Donnie said.

V smiled as she responded, “You will, Donnie, you will.”

Mag raised his hand and said, “I’ve told you about our UN recognition, but I also want to give you our newest project which V and I want Donnie and Louise to lead us in the coming years. If they agree to do so, they will create over the next year, hopefully with Carnegie Mellon and the University of Pittsburgh AI systems, a viable monitoring system to put binders of sort on AI to remain computer oriented and within the control of humans. It will be a challenge, but we have had many over our years together. This one will touch, not only our country, but the world, our world. But I believe it’s critical to bring all AI forces together to come up with an internationally acceptable method of making sure humanity maintains control of the functions of AI. Now let me know what you think about this proposal and if Donnie and Louise will offer their services to do so."

Donnie leaned over to Louise, and they talked for a few seconds, then he stood up and said, "We got it. We'll do it and meet with all you guys and gals after this session and talk over a plan for us to work together. Once we're done with a preliminary outline, we'll all come back with you, Mag and V, to go over our initial plan. Let me add, I think you are right on, and it is critical to put a plan together."

Mag smiled and said, "What more could V and I expect from you two and all of you. It will be a macro program which we will all work on in the coming year and probably beyond," as he looked over at V and added, "Anything you want to add V?"

V smiled and said, "No, you guys nailed it. Whatever you need us from us, we'll do it. It is a proper program our boss man Mark would be so proud of us to do at this critical time. So, let's do it as we, you always have."

Mag then looked out at the others and said, "Well that is a terrific goal for us in the coming year and I am excited, again, as usual, by you all," as he paused, looked at his watch and said, "You know we need a break because we got a lot more to go over but I think it's time we get into our circle as we did that first night, what, fifteen years ago, and celebrate a life: Mark's and now our own. So let's celebrate our lives and all the lives we have helped over the ensuing years," he said, then laughed, smiling. "You know fifteen years ago I would never have used that word, 'ensuing.' I would have thought it was some type of lawsuit."

The roar rumbled through them all as they moved together to form a circle. Around the circle it was silent, only a few voices from the area of the bar. The young folks in the circle stood silent with head's down, then they looked up as Mag raised his fist toward them. In his deep voice he said, "Here's to you Mark, I know you're watching us." Then he took V's hand and waved at the others to join them. The others walked closer to Mag and V and formed a tighter circle with smiles across their faces.

"Okay, let's go," Mag said, as they connected with their hands, "but I want to add what I was just talking about that Mark would say at a time like this. Each day is a life he would say, so let's live it and help others do the same. Okay, got that?"

Mag and V begin the slogan slowly and the other's joined in unison, "Each day is a life, so let's live it as best we can and help others do the same."

THE END

ABOUT THE AUTHOR

Dave Borland is a writer of novels, poetry, short stories, and plays. He is a graduate of West Virginia University with an English Major, and is a native of Pittsburgh.

Over the past 25 years Dave has written a variety of stories which express his visual, emotional, and personal reflections of life in these early days of the 21st Century.

His writings focus on overcoming the negative fears of society worldwide by having positive characters of mixed ages and backgrounds overcome todays' issues with their personal, creative, positive and AI-created solutions.